Christopher Tilghman
The Way People Run
Stories

One of America's finest writers, the author of *Mason's Retreat* ("Magnificent"—*Publishers Weekly*) and *In a Father's Place* ("Radiant"—*The New York Times*), now gives us a stunning new collection of short stories.

In these remarkable short stories, the writer who has been compared to John Cheever, William Maxwell, and Wright Morris once again creates brilliant fiction about the fault lines that crack open in people, marriages, and families. Against the backdrop of vivid American settings—the Chesapeake Bay region and the American West—Chris Tilghman writes with humor and generosity about the many ways that people try to run away from themselves and the lives they've created. The title story was chosen by Robert Stone for *The Best American Short Stories*, and another story here was chosen by Tobias Wolff to appear in another *Best American Short Stories* volume. The deep emotional connections, and disconnections, between people and within people's inner lives are at the heart of these magnificent stories by a modern American master.

Praise for Christopher Tilghman:

"Echoes of *The Great Gatsby*, William Styron's *Lie Down in Darkness*, O'Neill, and Faulkner...a stunning individual achievement."
—*Kirkus Reviews*

"*Mason's Retreat* is a brilliant book—full of wisdom and insight into the workings of the soul....Every paragraph holds a treasure. This is one of the most thoroughly satisfying novels you will ever read."
—Kaye Gibbons

Christopher Tilghman is a recipient of a Guggenheim Fellowship, the Whiting Writer's Award, and the Ingram Merrill Foundation Award. His fiction has appeared in *The New Yorker*. He lives in Massachusetts with his wife and three sons.

PUBLICITY
Author tour: Boston, Baltimore, Washington, D.C., Iowa City, San Francisco

ADVERTISING
The New York Times Book Review

PREVIOUS BOOKS
In a Father's Place
cloth: 0-374-17558-6 (FS&G)
paper: 0-312-15553-0 (Picador)

Mason's Retreat
paper: 0-614-27291-2 (Picador)

Fiction
224 pp • 5½ x 8¼
0-679-44971-X
$21.00/C$32.00

W9-BLV-531

ALSO BY CHRISTOPHER TILGHMAN

Mason's Retreat
In a Father's Place

THE WAY PEOPLE RUN

THE WAY

STORIES

Christopher Tilghman

PEOPLE RUN

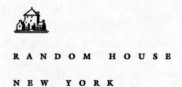

RANDOM HOUSE

NEW YORK

Copyright © 1999 by Christopher Tilghman

All rights reserved under International and Pan-American
Copyright Conventions.Published in the United States by
Random House, Inc., New York, and simultaneously in Canada
by Random House of Canada Limited, Toronto.

RANDOM HOUSE and colophon are registered trademarks
of Random House, Inc.

All of the stories in the collection are works of fiction. Names, characters, places,
and incidents are the product of the author's imagination or are used fictitiously.
Any resemblance to actual events, locales, or persons, living or dead, is entirely
coincidental.

Some of these stories have appeared in earlier form in the following magazines and
anthologies: "Something Important" in *The Boston Globe Sunday Magazine;* "A
suitable Good-bye" in *The Yale Review;* "The Way People Run" in *The New
Yorker* and in *The Best American Short Stories, 1992;* "Things Left Undone" in *The
Southern Review* and in *The Best American Short Stories, 1994.* The author thanks
the editors for their close attention and valuable suggestions, and also Maxine
Groffsky and Kate Medina, for their support and guidance from the first words to
the last.

Library of Congress Cataloging-in-Publication Data
Tilghman, Christopher.
    The way people run : stories / Christopher Tilghman. — 1st ed.
        p. cm.
    ISBN 0-679-44971-X
    1. United States—Social life and customs—20th century—Fiction. 2. Eastern
Shore (Md. and Va.)—Social life and customs—Fiction.
    I. Title.
PS3570.I348W39 1999
813'.54—dc21   98-33888

Random House Website address: www.atrandom.com

Printed in the United States of America on acid-free paper

9 8 7 6 5 4 3 2

First Edition

Book design by Victoria Wong

To my mother,
Elizabeth Forbes Morison

Contents

THE WAY PEOPLE RUN

Something Important

Peter Ramsey was spending a few days with his brother, Mitch, in an old family cottage on the Rappahannock when he learned that his wife was sleeping with another man. He was in that place with that company because Mitch had called him early one morning and asked him to come, had told him that they had to get together, the two of them, and "dialogue." Peter had not seen him or heard from him directly in at least three years. "Aunt Eliza's cottage. Sometime in the next couple of days," Mitch had argued. "Just wait for me."

Peter hung up, and told Eileen what he had said. She had been running around the bedroom madly getting dressed for the day, but when she figured out who was making this call at dawn, she stopped and stood where she could listen. Peter whistled, as if nothing he'd ever heard made less sense than meeting Mitch at the cottage.

Eileen said, "He's your brother, after all," as if there had ever been a time in forty-two years that he had not known that.

"I've got work to do."

"Honestly, you can work there as well as here." It was true enough: Peter taught high school English and his single task for the summer was preparing a new course in the Russian novel. "The first time he calls you in years there must be something up."

Peter arrived at the cottage the next evening. The moist air inside surprised him, as if the mildew should have been finished with the place years ago and left it blanched and dry. It was a simple structure, an old herdsman's residence long since cut off from its farm, but there was a broad porch across the water side that looked out the creek toward the slow Rappahannock emptying into the Bay. When Peter thought of his great-aunt Eliza, he remembered her on this porch, only half sitting on the edge of a wicker settee. She was a maiden lady from Louisville, restless enough with her lot to have loved this modest, unassuming place. When he thought of her he remembered pins, cameo brooches, and antique pearls, because her dress was never complete until she had gathered a fistful of material across her fallen, sunken chest.

He slept soundly that night, soothed by the light clatter of tulip leaves outside his window, his cheek on Aunt Eliza's monogrammed pillowcase, English linen that smelled clean as a wheat field but still seemed slightly damp, as if a lover had been sleeping there. He was awakened around four by noises coming from the creek, a diesel engine gargling and a radio that seemed close enough to whisper to him. He looked out through the branches and saw the dark silhouette of a work boat stretched out across the break in the water elms and pines. The running lights drew an even green line on the black horizon. He could make out the waterman, standing at his helm, illuminated by the ochre dials of the control panel, and could almost smell the hot coffee, could feel the greasy dew on the canvas decking. The boat cut out of the sleep of the creek hollow and headed toward the river's open water, leaving behind the strains of exhaust and country music.

In the morning he dragged a brocaded chair and a marble-topped table out onto the porch and set up the books and notes he was using to put together his new seminar. An exuberant rush of concentration soon gave way to the distractions of air fragrant with the raw life of low tide, and the distant sounds of men working the outdoors. About ten he heard the hum of an approaching vehicle, and was almost disappointed to think it must be Mitch, on time, but it was a coarse sound and it turned out to be a farmer on a tractor come to mow the field between the house and creek. Peter could not imagine by what arrangement the farmer did this. Perhaps it was a courtesy or a contract that had outlived Aunt Eliza, but if the farmer did it for pay, it was certain that he did not get his money from Mitch. Who, wondered Peter, having once done business with Mitch, would ever trust him again?

Peter worked into the middle of the afternoon, stopping only a few times to look at his watch and speculate whether Mitch would arrive at all. As the sun began to fall upriver, he left his desk and walked the expanse to the water. In his childhood he had passed days on this shoreline, making villages of twigs and grass. He could not remember how Mitch spent his time at Aunt Eliza's. He wondered, not for the first time, whether one of them was adopted, or whether at least they did not share the hopeless, ill man that both of them had called Dad. Growing up, Mitch had looked and acted and in fact played linebacker on their Country Day football team; Peter was thin and tall, with dark curly hair, gawky as a boy and still slightly insubstantial. But then he heard a shout from the house, and it was a voice so familiar, so much a part of him, that it seemed to come not through his ears but through his blood.

"Hey, asshole."

Mitch was standing a few yards into the field, framed between the two arching tulip trees. He was rounder now, and he appeared an unhealthy and unnatural pink in the afternoon light. He was wearing a baggy pair of red Bermudas that hung off his gut; everything about him seemed heavy—the fabric of his extra-large polo shirt, which hung like chain mail, the pair of thick sunglasses swinging on a cord around his neck. Peter crossed the field, eyes down at the clumps of fresh-cut hay; he waved once halfway.

"You made it," said Peter, putting out his hand. To his dismay, he saw that Mitch was raising both of his bulky arms.

"Gotta give the little brother a hug," said Mitch, explaining the awkward closing of bodies that took place.

Peter took a step back. "You made it," he said again, this time making it plain that he was referring to all the times in the past when Mitch had not.

Mitch paid no attention to the churlish tone. "Some business came up at the last minute. I'm just glad you're here, old boy."

"So what's up?" asked Peter. "I hope nothing bad."

Mitch might have begun to answer, but at that moment Peter heard a rustling by the edge of the house, and looked up to see a woman walking toward him with a wide smile on her face. She had a large pair of sunglasses perched on her blond head, and her white canvas sailor pants were so tight he could see the perfect outline of her blue underpants. Her aging skin showed the result of too many days on the beach. He did not have to ask Mitch who she was; over the years he had brought dozens of girlfriends and women into the most private family moments, starting back in their teens the time a photographer was hired to take candids of Aunt Eliza's eightieth. When the proofs came back, even Mitch couldn't remember the name of the eager, tactless face that seemed to appear in every scene.

"*This* is Margaret," said Mitch, and Peter knew the accent was covering lies he had told her: *My brother can't wait to meet you; Mother said to give you her best.* Peter did not want to hurt her feelings, so he smiled weakly and began to walk around to the front of the cottage as if there were some business he had to attend to. The grille of a car came into view, and it was a big fancy Volvo. Mitch always had a new car, even when it sounded as if he were living at a Y somewhere; he was the first person Peter had ever heard of who leased a car, and to this day Peter considered leasing to be one more strategy for living beyond one's means. But the car was not the worst of it, because as Peter rounded the corner the next thing he saw was a boat on a trailer, a small day sailer with a mast slung on a cradle overhanging the car.

"This boat," he yelled at Mitch, who had followed him. "Where the hell did you get this boat?"

"Hey," he said. "I rented it from some marina up the road." He tried to humor Peter. "We can't be here without a *boat.*"

Aunt Eliza never had a boat; they never sailed there. "I thought you were in trouble or something. I've been here waiting and you show up with a girlfriend and a goddamned boat!"

Mitch didn't know what to do. They hadn't squared off

like this since they used to play Ping-Pong; they kept score, sort of, but the real object was to hit the other guy with the ball and hurt him. Peter watched his brother visibly searching for—and failing to find—any plausible reason that he should be attacked in this way. Mitch had a gift for appearing victimized; it was always his final card, and so often it worked. It was working, finally, on Peter, because he looked away and his eye landed again on the boat, such an innocently cheerful sight and shape, like a picnic basket. A slight breeze rattled through the leaves above, an invitation to sail. He could suddenly picture Mitch driving up here with Margaret, rolling absently through farmlands and through the old church-and-theater towns of the Tidewater. They begin to pick up strands of the river, and "WHOA," yells Mitch, surprising Margaret. "A BOAT!" he says, and they loop around the divided highway and back toward a boatyard, and there is no lack of trailer hitch or money or sailing experience in Mitch's mind to compete with the image of genteel summer weekday sailing at Aunt Eliza's. It's only after he and Margaret have resumed the road that he admits to himself, as he has denied to the boat owner so successfully, that he is a beginner in a sailboat, a novice, but a great liar.

Peter shook his head and reached out to give the boat a tap. "Asshole," he said. He helped Mitch and Margaret unpack the car; she worked purposefully and seemed uninterested in the brotherly contentions. Peter nosed through the grocery bags that Mitch had brought, and he found all the familiar brands and foods—brothers, no matter what, shared the same table—but Mitch as always had bought the large size, the family size, and three of everything, as if a good time could be built on several pounds of solid white tunafish in spring water. Peter remembered Mitch in their teenage years, shopping for a weekend ski trip or camping trip. He could see him proceeding up and down the supermarket aisles, his cart a wide maw: *Load it up; no sense in doing without; hey, it's vacation.* Mitch would pay for it all; his wallet had always seemed fat and heavy. But after the show in the supermarket the thick wallet would not reappear during that weekend in the mountains or at the beach, and when Peter made the last silent tally of expenses, it was clear that food had been the least of them.

Peter finished putting the food away, popped a beer, and went out to the porch. He heard Mitch and Margaret before he saw them, way out on the piney point stretching into the river. A tour of the sights, especially out to the point, was part of the arrival at Aunt Eliza's. In the days after the battle of Fredericksburg, the people on the neck had gone out there to count swollen blue and gray bodies floating into the Bay. There were all sorts of stories: a deserter, naked of allegiance, swimming for home; two brothers, in rival uniforms, washed up in rigid embrace. Peter could hear Mitch telling her these ridiculous tales, and as nothing else, they charmed him, Aunt Eliza's private store of American history. By the time Mitch and Margaret reappeared at the bottom of the field Peter had drunk three beers, and as he stood for their approach he could feel the thinning and softening of his blood.

"We were scouting out a place to launch the boat," said Mitch, after he had showered, put on a Hawaiian shirt, and settled into a chair beside Peter. He pointed toward a spot at the lower corner of the field. "Easy," he announced, and took a very long drink of beer, belching slightly at the end. He gave his mouth a stagey wipe with the back of his hand, and then motioned out over the water toward the low band of the opposite bank, a world apart, an hour away by car. "Best sight in the world," he said, as if he owned everything he saw.

Peter turned and apologized for yelling at him.

"No problem," said Mitch.

Peter knew it would be no problem with Mitch; forgiveness was easy for him, something to be encouraged all around. "I mean I really want to apologize to Margaret. I didn't mean she was unwelcome. I just didn't expect her."

"So I gathered," said Mitch. "How's Eileen?"

Peter was surprised and slightly irritated to hear Mitch use her name. "She's fine," he answered quickly. "You haven't seen her in years," he added.

"I was hoping she'd come."

"Mitch, you didn't exactly present this as a family re-union. You said it was important." From behind him, in the kitchen, he could hear Margaret hunting through the unfamiliar cabinets.

"So how's business," he said. For many years this was the one question that he was afraid, or simply embarrassed, to ask. He watched as Mitch made a stylized show of pulling out his wallet, selecting a business card, and handing it over. Peter read it, and it was as anonymous, as un-revealing, as a forged passport. "BSR Associates," it said. The address was Orlando; the last time he knew, Mitch was in Dallas. "What does BSR Associates do?" he asked.

"Oh. The usual mix. Waste management and financial services."

They both fell silent, and Peter watched the wood-boring wasps disappearing into the porch rail. A fat wood-chuck down by the water made a waddling dash to the trees, and Mitch brought the shape of a rifle to his shoulder and squeezed off a round. The long, flat call of a blue heron stretched across the creek, which was slowly be-coming amber in the low western light.

"We need crabs," said Mitch suddenly. "I told Margaret we'd get a bushel." He pronounced it "boo-shul," like the watermen, like, in fact, Aunt Eliza, who picked up occasional Tidewater pronunciations and took pleasure in using them back in Louisville.

"How 'bout another beer?" Peter asked, getting up.

Mitch didn't answer, but simply heaved his empty can out onto the grass and then held one hand forward for a cold one. "This is freedom," he said.

Peter found Margaret in the kitchen standing on a chair, peering back into the recesses of a top shelf. He could see the taut muscles stretching through her calves and up into the full skirt of a purple cotton sundress. When she saw him she gave up and smiled; she wasn't very pretty—petite women with upturned noses like Margaret don't seem to age all that well—but she was radiant with health and good will.

"I wanted to say I'm sorry," he said. "I was being childish and rude."

She climbed down from her chair and gave him a generously open smile. She began breaking lettuce into a china bowl, and Peter leaned back as if they would now have a chance to begin over, but they were instantly interrupted by Mitch bellowing from the porch. "Driiiink."

They looked at each other and smiled again, and Peter saw Mitch behind her expression, good old dumb, affable Mitch; he knew instantly that she loved that man as anyone must love another, from the inside out. He did not know anything about them, how long they had been together, where she lived, but it seemed to Peter that he was past asking any of this sort of background question; they were in-laws now, supportive in-laws, admitting the fact of family failings but without prying too far into the details.

Margaret would fight someone who judged Mitch too harshly—Peter could see that; she'd fight Mitch's brother, if it ever came to it—but she'd rather simply be in a place where nobody was expected to be perfect. Peter winked and went to the refrigerator. They went back out to the porch together and they all sat in a line in the oddly matched assemblage of furniture, with Margaret in the middle.

The evening that settled on them was soft and sweet; the river and Bay were dead calm. It was not most people's idea of a vacation spot; instead of the slap of seawater heavy with minerals, the Chesapeake offered a flaccid, tepid flow, a mild brackishness dotted with jellyfish. Not most people's idea of fun, but good enough for Aunt Eliza, thought Peter; good enough for me.

Mitch pointed to the spot he had earlier designated for launching the boat. "That's where we're going to launch her," he said.

"So you had announced," said Peter, with some sarcasm in his voice, but Mitch had always lived beyond the reach of sarcasm anyway. Peter was getting drunk, and he had started to feel a rush of pleasure at being here with Mitch and Margaret, and without Eileen. It had begun to feel like vacations never felt anymore, release into some new world. It was ten-thirty by the time they sat down to eat at the broad mahogany table jammed into the small Victorian parlor. They opened a bottle of white wine that no one needed, and with the first sip Peter knew he had stepped over the line. Margaret's eyes were starting to look tired and very much over forty, maybe even fifty, and Mitch was nodding off like the uncle at Christmas dinner. Peter hadn't been drunk like this in years, and by God, it seemed it was different at middle age, far less fun and much too mortal. He looked around the room, at Margaret and Mitch, at Aunt Eliza's things, at his own hands, smelled the char of burned chicken and the foul film of beer on his breath, and it all began to feel rather arbitrary, as if there were no past after all, and as if he could, and maybe should, let go any time he liked.

He woke in the morning after a fitful night, going to the bathroom a few times and then, on schedule, waking for the waterman as he passed them by. It was the ringing of the telephone that finally got him up, and he staggered downstairs in his boxer shorts. He was surprised to see Margaret, already dressed, holding the receiver out to him. It was Eileen.

"Who was that?"

"Margaret," he said. "A friend of Mitch's."

"What's going on there? Has Mitch spoken to you?"

"What do you mean? We've been talking."

There was a pause, a long pause and Peter could think of absolutely nothing to say, so he waited for her.

"I thought Mitch had something to tell you."

"I don't know." It was the honest answer. "Don't cross-examine me," he added quickly. Margaret had graciously left the room to give him some privacy, but he knew he could still be heard all over the house. "I'm sure I'll get a chance to talk to Mitch this morning."

"It sounds like a house party," said Eileen.

"I guess it does," he said, but even as hungover as he felt, he was glad to be one of the guests.

"So you won't be home tonight?"

"Probably not," he said, with the vague feeling that she had been checking on him as if she did not trust him with Mitch. "No. I won't be," he added definitively, and they hung up.

He looked around the kitchen and could see that he was not only the last one up, but that the others had eaten big meals, eggs and scrapple, English muffins. Outside, from down at the water, he heard the clank of metal and the sound of voices, and he opened the screen door to look out. Mitch had backed his boat and Volvo deep into the cattails and seemed to be trying to get the boat ready. Peter gazed up into the treetops and there wasn't a breath of wind; the morning was so slack it hung in front of his eyes in sheets of powdery haze. He figured he might well throw up yet, but instead of standing there waiting for it, he put on his jeans and stumbled across the field.

"Did you get his license plate?" called Mitch; the old jokes of their father's still seemed satisfactory to him.

"Shit," said Peter.

"No. It's 'she-it.' " He turned to Margaret. "Peter never learned how to swear. You can tell right away he doesn't mean it."

Mitch had backed the Volvo as far as possible into the shore grasses; the trailer had come to a jolting stop against the hidden remains of a concrete seawall. The lens of one of the taillights lay shattered, a brilliant red mistake on the marshy floor. Mitch was standing waist deep in the grass alongside the boat, holding a handful of ropes and apparently trying to thread one of them the length of the mast. It would be difficult, even if he knew what he was doing, but there would have been no time to wait for instruction when he rented the boat, just a "Sure. Sure. Do you take plastic?" Mitch's boat. It was starting to get touching. And because of that, it seemed suddenly to matter, mattered enough for Peter to swallow back the last heave of his stomach and wade into the tangle. Once they mastered the rigging they turned their attention to the hull, and soon discovered that as compact as the boat looked, and as preferable as fiberglass was to wood, it took all their combined strength to slide it off the trailer. It came to a stop, foundering on the seawall. They assembled a selection of levers from the orderly line of driftwood snaking through the dense cordgrass, but they could do little but peel off spirals of fiberglass on the sharp edges of the concrete.

"Try to take the weight off your end," said Mitch. Peter

was only able to rock the boat some more; the sound was becoming the worst part of the project, the chewing and scraping that resonated from the hull like a massive sounding board. Mitch leaned back for another of his frequent rests. "Wait," he said. "Gotta pace yourself."

"Let's just put it back on the trailer," said Peter.

Mitch looked at him with a great round show of amiable disbelief.

"It's not as if we ever sailed anyway."

"We always had a boat," said Mitch. The smile was gone, but now he was using the instructional tone of the older brother, the one who remembers better because he was there first. "It's family tradition."

One year, maybe, the Fergusons next door took them all for several excursions in their Chris-Craft, and the hunters who rented Aunt Eliza's duck rights let them use their aluminum duck boat for several years running, but that was it. "Come off it, Mitch."

"You always were a disagreeable little twerp," said Mitch, smiling broadly again.

Peter heard that familiar tone of voice, and helplessly he was back to when they were sixteen and twelve, and Mitch was calling him a disagreeable little twerp, and he was taking it with a cocky forced smile because he was unsure whether Mitch meant it or whether it was true. From then on, that was the way Mitch talked to him, as if they could only go that far together, as if they were frozen into their teenage years, as if they could never be real friends because they knew each other too well too young.

He stood back to look once more at their plight, and this time when they put their shoulders on it—screw the fiberglass—Peter exploded. After five minutes of increasingly unfocused shoving the boat was unmoved. The rotund curve, the acrid smell of it, the absurd benches in the cockpit; he now truly hated the whole thing, especially after he had lost control and had kept shoving alone long after Mitch started to yell "Hold it, hold it!"

"What about some lunch?" It was Margaret's voice. Peter had forgotten entirely about her; he wondered how long she had been watching. He stood panting for a minute or two.

"Fine. Hell with it," he said, and walked off toward the cottage, the low mumble of their voices slowly getting lost in the high sounds of summer and the swish of his slashing strides through the cut hay.

He was on the porch when he heard Mitch start up the Volvo, and he looked in time to see the wheels racing and clods of spongy soil being splattered against the boat hull, which now looked comical, a cartoon drawing of a shipwreck. The wheels caught finally and Mitch bounced out of the shore grass, his bulky body seeming to fill the entire glass area as he was launched by the hummocks. He turned left to follow the road back up the neck without stopping.

"I'm sorry," Peter called out to Margaret once again, as she walked up. "All I've done since you got here is apologize," he said.

She sat beside him on the top step. "I guess the two of you don't get to be alone together very much," she said.

No one who knew anything at all about the two of them would make such a comment. Peter's first impulse was to protest that it was so rare that it had never, since they were adults, happened at all. "Sure. Well, anyway, I'm sorry."

"Mitchell has been planning this trip for weeks," she stated. She was not above making him squirm a little. "I was afraid he wouldn't come without me," she added. "You know. He gets distracted." She gave the quickest nod in the direction he had driven.

Once again, Peter saw the meeting between them built upon what Aunt Eliza, with the greatest love, used to call Mitch's ways. "Why did he come? What's this all about?"

"You'll have to ask him."

"How is his business? Do you know?" He tried not to sound ironic.

"I think it's going very well. His partner was once a garbageman. I mean that literally. But this waste management thing is really going well."

They sat quietly for a moment and listened to the powerful buzzing of the locusts and the sounds of work that carried all the way from the waterman's boat far out in the river mouth.

"It's beautiful here," she said. "I took a wonderful walk around the shoreline. All those coves and points must have been fun for a child. I always envied people like you. I think I still do."

"Why?" Peter leaned toward her a little.

"With a big family. And all this history." She motioned out over the lawn, and up the creek toward the Rappahannock.

"It was just Aunt Eliza," he blurted out. "She bought this place to get away from Louisville and then invented a family to go with it."

"It's funny about you Southerners," she said. "Someone says family to you and you assume they mean generations. Family to me can happen in a single night."

"You didn't have any kind of a family life?"

"Not like you. Not like you and Mitchell. He has told me so much about all your adventures."

Peter had been taken by surprise before by information that came back to him from Mitch, events that they had supposedly shared but were absolute news to him, or were just a dimly perceptible skeleton for anecdotes that were utter fiction. "Like what?" he asked.

"Oh," she said carefully, "he told me he knocked your two front teeth out when you were five, with a frozen Snickers bar. Can that be true?" She brought both hands to her mouth and paused. "And I love the story about that night in Paris when the two of you and some friends split up and kept on stealing each other's cars. Mitch says he never laughed as hard as when he caught you at dawn carrying the driver's seat of his Renault across the square in front of Notre Dame. It really is a funny picture."

"Yes," said Peter. It was one of his own favorite memories.

"Hey, Twerps!" Mitch's voice came from behind the house, over the rumble, clank, and an occasional jolt of steel of an approaching tractor. When it came into view Peter was not surprised to see Mitch riding high on the mudguard like a farm-belt politician. Over the engine noise he was carrying on a conversation with the driver. On the back of the tractor was a backhoe, and with a few canvas straps under the hull, and a raising of the backhoe boom, the work with the boat was quickly done. Mitch and the farmer parted with an easy laugh. Peter watched to see if the hand reached back for the fat wallet, but it did not.

By this time Margaret had changed into her bathing suit and had packed a Playmate full of drinks. Peter ran back to the house and peeled off his sweaty clothes with the sudden fear that they might leave without him. He pulled on a pair of shorts and a T-shirt. His legs were untanned and mottled with imperfections, but even from the porch Mitch's torso was so vibrantly pale that it looked as if he had been pressure-treated in preservative. Mitch and Margaret were in the boat and waiting when he got back, and Mitch was sitting with the tiller in his hand and a captain's hat on his head. It had a white top with an embroidered anchor and chain, but it was at least a size too small for Mitch's buffalo head, and the price tag remained on the shiny black bill.

Peter walked the boat away from shore through a patch of water celery, and gave a last shove seaward as he leaped over the side into the cockpit seat opposite Margaret. They drew away from the land slowly, a slight confusion of bubbles in the wake, a trickling under the hull in the still air. It wasn't really hot yet—it was still June. A water snake, its head only a thumb on the serene surface, sinuated past them, ducking under once when Mitch waved his hat. Peter looked back and watched the trees and points crossing each other slowly, a layering of familiar features that soon became just a line of green. His hand trailed in the water. It was silent, but there were occasional freshets of air, sensible to the boat as it hopped skittishly across the Rappahannock.

"This is the life," said Mitch. He was facing forward on the low seat, leaning over his gut and legs. The captain's hat, surprisingly, gave him a touch, almost, of dignity. Margaret was stretched out the length of the cockpit on one side.

"Ready about . . . hard a lee," said Mitch. Peter glanced up in some surprise to hear these nautical terms, and saw that using them made Mitch smile, but the boat was som-nolent, and the sail simply sagged in the middle.

"In irons," Mitch announced. "This is pisser."

"Quite the salt," said Peter. It was clear that somewhere along the line Mitch had taken a sailing lesson or two.

Margaret raised one eye slightly above the side and took a bearing on where they were; she looked as if she had woken from a dream, slightly startled and then quickly re-assured. She rearranged a towel under her head and closed her eyes again. Between the water and sky the land was as flat as a pencil line; Peter could no longer distinguish the mouth of their creek.

"We've got to get here more often," said Mitch.

"Well that's right," said Peter, suddenly reminded of the whole reason for this trip. "Why did you come? Is now a time to talk?" he said, nodding slightly toward Margaret's dozing form.

"Oh, hell," said Mitch, shrugging. He avoided Peter with a glance up at the sail. "Hard to say," he added, and as soon as this last phrase came out Margaret's eyes opened with the sudden intensity of spotlights.

"Mitchell," she said.

Poor Mitch, thought Peter, skewered out here on the water where he can't run. Time for Mitch to make one of his confessions, another impropriety with some small fam-ily bank account that supposedly they shared. Peter began to feel very sorry for him, especially because Margaret was not going to let him off the hook, which seemed unnecessary here on this floating diversion. *Drink your beer and let the bastards be.* That was one of the few useful things Peter could recall his father ever saying.

"The thing is, Peter, Mother thinks you're unhappy."

"What?"

"Mother. You know. Watching out for her little flock." Mitch tried to laugh.

"That's it?"

"That's what?"

"That's why I came here? So you could pass along that message? Mother tells me that herself on the phone, a couple of times a week."

Mitch suddenly looked a little hurt; Peter could see that he was thinking back to the last several weeks to see if she called him so often.

"Just because someone takes life seriously it doesn't mean he's unhappy," said Peter.

Mitch held up his hands, deflecting the charge. "I'm not trying to change the way you live, you know."

"You don't know how I live anyway."

Mitch responded thoughtfully. "We haven't been in touch lately as much as we should. Perhaps I'm as much to blame as anyone."

" 'As anyone'? There's only two of us, Mitch."

"You're the English professor," he said. "You know what I mean."

Peter did know what Mitch meant. He had not exactly been sending Mitch a stream of newsy letters. But the conversation seemed to have ended at this pass. Mitch appeared content to let it drift off with the tide, and Peter could begin to relax. *Who the hell are they—Mitch and Mother—to say I'm unhappy? Let's get real here.* But even as he used these thoughts to regain his balance, he knew they were not the complete truth, and when Margaret restarted the discussion with an impatient and communicative clearing of her throat, he had little in reserve.

Mitch and Margaret exchanged glances, and he sighed deeply. "See, the real question is . . ." They were getting to the bottom line, and as late in the game as it was, Peter still considered it possible that it would all come back to some problem or trouble of Mitch's. "How are things on the home front? That's the real question."

The answer burst forward. "My marriage? You're asking about me and Eileen? I don't get this at all." He wanted to take a big slashing swing at Mitch; *he* had been divorced once and could very possibly and probably have been married and divorced a couple more times without anyone finding out. But now Mitch was peeking out at him under the plastic visor of his captain's hat, and his eyes were saying *I've got my fingers crossed. Whatever I'm saying, I'm saying because the women are making me.*

"Mother says the last time you visited she seemed distant."

The last time they visited in Louisville, at Christmas-
time, he and Eileen were in the middle of deciding
whether she should take a new job in New York. She
wanted to; he didn't. "She seemed a little distant because
she was. We were making some decisions."

"Hey," said Mitch. "Relax, okay?"

Peter tried to take this advice, but he could feel his chest
and shoulders tightening into a clench. "There's nothing
wrong with our marriage," he said without thinking.
"Maybe we have to work on our relationship. I don't
know."

"Well, that's right," said Mitch with a full, round air of
conclusion, almost with a tone of congratulation to both
of them for getting through this conversation intact.
"Who doesn't have to work on the old 'home relationship'?"

Peter debated once more taking the offense; it was difficult, on these matters, to accept a fellowship with Mitch.
But would he argue that he and Eileen were having a wonderful time these days? That they laughed a lot, went to
movies, saw friends, lived the free life of a childless couple
well established and well paid enough to see the world?

The conversation was over for Mitch, anyway. For the
past few minutes he had been heading home, and the wind
had begun to cooperate. He shielded his eyes under his
hat's small brim and put on a reasonable rendition of a
waterman's discerning scowl. "We must get a bushel of

crabs," he said. "Goddamn vacation isn't complete without a bushel taken right here."

Peter was ready to laugh at this, but in the very small
moment it took him to reflect on it, Margaret snapped up-
right and glared first at Mitch and then, surprisingly, at
Peter.

"Margaret?" said Mitch. "Dear?"

"Well it's none of my business," she said, but even she
could hardly swallow this disclaimer. As soon as she raised
the issue, Peter realized she had made everything her business. This gathering, in fact, was largely her doing.

Mitch said, "I'm telling Peter what's on my mind."

He looked for confirmation, and Peter nodded vigor-
ously. *Like my brother says,* he thought.

"Is that it? Is that all you're going to say?"

"Margaret invented the phrase 'Do you want to talk
about it?' " said Mitch, with a mimicking whine. "She can
change a lightbulb alone, but she thinks the lightbulb has
to want to change."

"Go to hell," she said. "Just *communicate,*" she added,
staring quite pointedly at Peter.

"Margaret is a big believer in the social niceties. You
know. Keep the love alive with Hallmark."

Peter tried to laugh but could only look away.

"Okay," said Margaret. "Do it your own way." She
reached for her shirt and pulled it over her head, thrusting
her arms through with a final show of emphasis. The
breeze had freshened considerably, as it often did on slack

days at dusk, just as the wind often died at dusk on days with a blow, a contrariness that was just one of many in this Chesapeake life. Mitch could truthfully appear to be giving the boat his complete attention, and he did it well, even if the landing was nothing more than a heavy drive up into the sand and grass. Margaret left without a word, and side by side they pulled the boat as far out of the water as they could, and began taking the mast down.

"What was that all about?" Peter asked finally, happy for the opportunity to talk about someone else's problems in love. But Mitch did not do what Peter expected, give a rueful grin, raise his arms in complete and utter confusion, and say "Chicks!" Instead, he settled his large pale eyes sadly on Peter, and this time, when he spoke, it was as if the man inside, clothed in the faults of his early years but wiser for the many mistakes these faults had caused him, was making a rare foray into the real world.

"It was about Eileen. About you and Eileen."

This time, Peter could not deflect Mitch with sarcasm, or cow him with rage, or still him with sullen silence. He looked down at the coil of rope in his hands, at the oily lap of water over his toes, and then sat heavily on the boat's shimmering deck. "What then?"

Mitch was miserable now and spoke incredulously. "Eileen really hasn't spoken to you, has she."

"About what? About this trip?" He clearly meant that she had not.

Mitch shrugged painfully, but the focus in his eyes remained strong. "It wasn't Mother that called me. It was Eileen. That's a first, I'll tell you," Mitch added, and his tone was not kind. "She's always treated me like I embarrassed her just asking for the salt."

Peter wanted to protest, but he could not. Yes, way back, before they were married, way back when they were college sophomores deeply and passionately in love, she first met Mitch and described him to their friends as a "card-carrying troglodyte." That had happened so long ago that Peter had forgotten until now that he was surprised by her mean joke and hurt that she would say this after Mitch, in his own misguidedly slick way, had tried so hard to charm her.

"Peter, I think she wants out."

"Is that what she said?"

"Frankly, it wasn't very coherent. Does she drink or anything?"

"No," answered Peter, but he knew why Mitch asked this and could hear her now: long, rambling introductory clauses, self-interruptions, asides and diversions. When she was nervous, she said "you know" about five times per sentence, and her voice became pinched and sharp. This was the reason she had decided to practice corporate law, and not litigation.

"She was talking about 'going through changes' and crap like that. I asked her if she wanted me to talk to you, like I had a clue what she was trying to say, and she jumped on it. I guess I figured she was going to tell you something and wanted me around to support you. The brother thing, I suppose."

Mitch let it go for a few minutes, absently gathering in ropes and sails while the winds continued to freshen behind him. Peter had his head held so low that his chin was touching his chest, and he could feel the thump of his heart right through his skull.

"I never expected that it was up to me to lay this all on you."

"It's okay," said Peter. "Who else would drive a thousand miles to do it?"

"I gotta say," said Mitch, "that I think her asking me to do this stinks. Am I allowed to say I find it a teeny bit less than first-rate?"

"Yes," said Peter.

Mitch waded over and put a hand on Peter's back. "I'm sorry. Thing is, nothing is certain. Just a bad patch, probably. You'll just have to get to work on it."

Peter felt that hand and heard these words, and both of them helped. This boat he sat on, it was Mitch's idea of a gift, not coming empty-handed to the hospital room, no need to sit around getting maudlin, for Christ's sake. Peter thumped on the deck and looked up at Mitch. "Thanks for this," he said. "And Margaret. Thanks for inviting her to . . . this."

"Hey," said Mitch.

"How are we going to get it out of the water?" he asked.

Mitch snapped his fingers and then blew across his palm as if he were distributing pixie dust over the cause of difficulty; it was another of their father's gags, performed with the old confidence. The strange thing was, if one looked only at the immediate crises in their father's life, and not the long-running one that *was* his life, it often worked. It was his own special magic, and Mitch had willingly inherited it.

"Tomorrow," Mitch said. "Poof."

Peter could see this boat, its ropes and spars dragging like entrails, lifting slowly out of the water and floating over the grass.

When they reached the cottage they found Margaret showered and dressed in sparkling white, a rather frilly Southern-belle outfit that Eileen would make fun of but Peter thought made her look beautiful. He could use a little of the old fashions just about now, and a little less of the severe lawyer's suits and other garments for women who took business trips. Margaret waved as they approached. She yelled out that the steaks were ready to put on, and after showers, the three of them sat again for supper: steaks, a salad, and red wine, all taken in moderation. Margaret knew she was being counted upon to be cheerful, and she carried the conversation through dinner; Peter recognized how hard it was to do this, and that she must have had to do it often to be so good at it. Lord knew what her life had been like. Mitch was quiet through dinner, becoming an alarming red with sunburn, bad enough to make him sweat in the evening's chilly breeze. They did the dishes together, the three of them in the small kitchen, and then Margaret and Mitch said good night.

"I'm going to call Eileen," he said.

Mitch and Margaret traded looks: there was no need for subterfuge, but time now to give room for respect. Margaret headed up the narrow cottage stairs, and Mitch paused to place his hand once again on Peter's shoulder, and to say, "I'm going to get us some crabs. That is the key to your life over the next twenty-four hours."

Peter waved his brother off and poured himself another glass of wine. He dialed Eileen's work number; she was always working, would always be working. But the night operator came back this time after fifteen minutes and said she was not there. Peter called home, and there was no answer. It was eight-fifteen, and an unanswered telephone meant nothing, absolutely nothing, even if Eileen's voice on the other end would, in fact, have meant something. He knew now why she had encouraged him so strongly to come here, to come see the brother who had been for so long invisible to her; he suspected now that she had done it for another reason: to engineer two nights to herself. He dialed at nine, and when he dialed again at ten he had already begun to ask himself, in a way that was astonishingly abstracted, whether he really wanted to know. To see into the dark and forbidden world of another's dream life, his own wife's fantasies as she lay in bed on Sunday morning, her husband in the shower, her nightgown drawn to her waist. He dialed at eleven, and the knot in his gut was robbing him of feeling, even of control, and he remembered his old college roommate telling him that he wet his pants the moment he discovered that his wife had gone to California supposedly to see her sister and had taken her diaphragm. Peter left the kitchen and went to the porch; he longed for Mitch and Margaret to be there, not just the black vacant coolness of empty chairs and a small double swing moving enough to squeak the chain. Peter heard above a heavy weight rolling in the too short and too narrow Victorian twin. He went back to the kitchen and sat down in the straight-backed wooden chair, and even dozed a bit. He woke up with an erection, as if images and fears were giving off some kind of musk. For a few minutes his body felt bony and dry with desire, an electric pulse in his mouth, his cheeks quivering. But this soon passed, leaving only the emptied vessel of another's victory. He looked around Aunt Eliza's kitchen almost as if he were once again a teenager, when similar hurts had all the feeling of death, without the permanence.

He went to bed, but he did not fall asleep. A few hours must have passed when he heard, in the darkened hall, the sound of someone leaving the house. And then it seemed only a minute until, far up the creek, a diesel fired to life, the first sounds a phlegmy cough, expelling carbon and air, a smell that seemed to fill his room as soon as the sound came in the window. Peter was out of his bed by the time he heard the first metallic scrape from the tinny radio speaker. He grabbed for his pants and sneakers as soon as the voices began to thread off the water, a voice he did not know and a voice he knew well. He was sprinting across the field on a broad intercept course as soon as the running lights sparkled through the pines and cut clear into view. The dew on his feet covered his ankles like a sock. He had reached the crumbled seawall when he finally made out Mitch's shape clearly in the deckhouse, alongside the waterman, each holding a cup of steaming coffee. They passed through the narrows opposite Peter, on the far side of the creek. He was yelling at them to give him a chance to wade over, but the rhythm of the conversation was not broken. Peter could not make out what they were saying, mostly because he kept yelling as they emptied past his point and headed almost majestically for open water, as if there was nothing wrong, and could never be any trouble, that couldn't be solved by a boo-shul of crabs.

Room for Mistakes

Over the past few years, Hal's unlikely stepfather, a former ranch hand named Roy, had seemed to be in failing health—his liver, maybe it was, or his pancreas, or some other residual damage from his drinking days. Hal's mother didn't go into details, and he didn't probe. When Roy finally died, that would be the end of a love story that had started when Hal was a small boy and had been running as the measure of his worth and empathy ever since. Hal was now two thousand miles away, in Newton, Massachusetts, and he expected that his next trip home to Montana would be for the funeral.

"I'd like us all to go," he announced to Marcie, though he doubted their daughters, one in law school and one in college, would be able to. "We owe him that, don't we?"

They were sitting in the kitchen, with Marcie lazily assembling a stew; he had poured himself a shot of bourbon and was sprawled at the round table, a large, slouching animal in this unnaturally neat space. Hal missed coming home to the gay disorder of a kitchen in a house with children, or at least the disarray of their kitchen when the girls were still at home, and when Marcie was teaching nursery school three days a week and serving as unofficial protector of projects and pets during vacations. But that seemed many, many years ago.

"You do," she said.

Hal nodded; he had been wrong about Roy and his intentions, back when his mother married him, and in the seven years since then had been trying to make amends. There was much about Roy and his past that no one knew, but what he had proven over the years was that he was a kind man and a redeemed soul who deserved to be remembered fondly at death. Hal's beef, after all, had been with his own late father and his mother, and with his brother, and hapless Roy had simply gotten in the way.

"Hal?" she said. He had fallen silent, recalling those days. Outside, an early December slush storm spattered momentary blobs of white on the black windows. "All I meant was that you really do owe him for what he has done for your mother. I'd go whether I owed him or not."

Hal let out a troubled sigh. He felt troubled often, these days; he was bored to death of being a banker. The only thing that kept his spirits up was the persistent rumor that his bank was about to be engulfed by Fleet; there would be consiolidations, cutbacks, early retirement options aplenty. In the meantime, he had taken to sudden infatuations. A few months ago he had impulsively purchased a new car, a tiny little Toyota RAV4, that was years too young for him; lately, he had decided it was time to take up kayaking, though as a boy raised in mountain ranch country, he could barely swim. Marcie supported these turns, telling their friends that "a new car is better than a bimbo," but she knew a new car was not enough.

"I wouldn't be so sure your mother will tell us," she said, picking up the conversation about Roy. "If I know Jean, she'll bury him and put the news in her Christmas card."

"Tidier, that way," said Hal, using his mother's favorite word.

"Exactly. No chance for anyone to snuffle and carry on all through his funeral service."

As he tossed and turned that night, Hal kept returning to images of home, a fevered outpouring of the senses: a roomful of men in cowboy boots, the tang of their sweat and clipped mumble of their voices; the suffocating but pure taste of hay chaff; the insistent smells of fresh paint and diesel oil in Millersburg back in the fifties, when America had won the war and its small heartland towns were reaping the rewards. Even as he fought to still his mind, he asked himself what this meant now, this dream-pull back to his boyhood; for nearly thirty years he had wondered if he would ever go back, to retire, maybe, or to escape some catastrophe in business or life. A few years ago their daughter Louisa had been critically ill with the same infection that killed Jim Henson, and for those few hours when it seemed that she really was going to die, at age fourteen, the only thing he could imagine doing afterwards was moving back to the ranch, as if he could pull a trapdoor over his grief.

He was now awake; he rarely slept through the night these days, and often prowled the house until dawn. He looked over at Marcie through the white shadows of a city bedroom lit by streetlamps; she slept peacefully in a soft feathering of gray hair. Fenway, their springer, came over to Hal, put his moist chin on his pillow, and exhaled warm, almost sweet, breath. Hal was glad for the company. Outside, he heard the thump of *The Boston Globe* and *The New York Times* landing on their front porch, the sound of a new day thrown at him from the dark, like a pair of dice.

When the word came, a few months later, it was not what either of them had expected. He was at work when his secretary put through a personal call, and he knew his mother had died as soon as it was Roy's voice he heard on the other end.

Her heart, in the night, never woke up. It was the way she did, had done, everything in her life: sudden, nonnegotiable, decided in advance. As he stood at his desk, Debbie drawn through his office door by the unmistakable pauses of bad news on the telephone, Hal felt as if he had known about her death for weeks.

He asked where her body was and what the plans were. "We'll catch a plane this afternoon," he said.

"You don't have to do that," said Roy. Roy explained that Jean had wanted to be cremated immediately, and then have her ashes spread from the high place above the ranch yard that the family called the Lookout. From that spot, the valley looked sweet, though the life people lived in that repetition of ranch yards and haylands was often bitter. Hal's father's ashes were there, as well as the graves of a few pets. "We can't do that until spring," Roy said. "Now's a tough season to travel anyway."

"Aren't we going to have a memorial service or something?"

"Folks won't expect you to come this time of year," he said, which was mostly true, as impossible as it was for Easterners to understand that weather and season can still impinge on people's lives. "Come when it's better out."

"But how about you, Roy. Are you okay? Wouldn't you need help?"

The voice on the other end faltered. Hal could picture the person that Roy was mourning, a much kinder person than Hal had ever known.

"Shannon's here," said Roy. "She can take care of it."

Shannon Avery, a woman from town who had done kitchen work for Jean as a teenager, had been helping them with errands and housework for the past few years. On their last visit, both Hal and Marcie had been struck by the way Shannon had inserted herself into the household, once lecturing Jean about her choice of groceries from the Safeway.

He hung up and looked over at Debbie. They had worked together for many years. Several times in one stretch they had come close to sleeping together—a simple nod from one or the other might have done it—and this phase had left behind an option of intimacy reserved for people with histories.

"Are you okay?" she asked. She was staring at him intently, which was discomfiting, as if he were being judged.

"Sure," he said.

"Thanks."

"Will you be leaving this afternoon?" She'd taken the precaution of bringing in his Week-at-a-Glance Calendar, though these days it was not as full as it had been in the past, when his bank's commercial lending had mattered to him more than it did now.

"No."

The questioning look remained on her face; her pen was still poised over the calendar. "Really?"

He explained what Roy had said, and added that Easterners never did understand how weather could affect one's plans. Debbie left, shaking her Catholic head; such a thing would never do in Dorchester. He called Marcie and told her about his mother, and after she had given herself a long pause and then blown her nose loudly into the receiver, she also asked if they would be leaving in the afternoon.

"I'm not sure," he said.

"You mean, ignore her death?"

"Of course not. I just got the impression that Roy didn't want us now. Maybe in a few weeks."

"That's odd," she said.

"No. Not really."

"Yes, really. Who's going to help with everything?"

He passed along what Roy had said: that Shannon was helping, had already made the arrangements for the cremation in Butte.

"Oh, great," said Marcie. "Do you really want Shannon Avery doing all that? Going through her things?"

Hal knew he'd better not admit it, but the thought of dealing with his mother's clothes made him shiver; he imagined overturning her underwear drawer into a cardboard box with his eyes closed. "It's how Roy wants to do it, I guess."

"You can't do this. It's the wrong thing to do."

He heard the cold sound of a moral judgment being passed on his deeds, and he responded accordingly. "Marcie, yours isn't the only way to grieve." He should have resisted giving this last statement an ironic flip, but his point was honest: He had loved his mother as his mother had loved him, from a distance.

"I'm not talking about grieving," Marcie snapped back. "If there's ever been a soul that can take care of itself, it's Jean's. I'm talking about you. Isn't it time to take care of all your baggage, for once and all?"

"Baggage. I thought it was just a life."

"Not for you, Hal. Your family, your past: you lug them around like a suitcase. Like it was chained to your wrist. There are questions here for you."

"Like which ones?"

"Well, what's going to happen to the ranch?"

"You mean, what's in Mom's will? Beats me. Maybe she's giving it to the Montana Militia."

"Be serious." She gave him a chance to say something, but when he didn't, she asked, "Aren't there cattle to feed, things like that?"

She was right about that, a practical matter if nothing else. He answered that all he had in mind was to wait a few weeks, as Roy had asked. "Nothing goes on at a cattle ranch in the middle of winter," he said, though he knew that in a month, at the very most, calves would be sprouting all over the place.

"Hal, I don't know what you're going to do with the place, but if you want it, any piece of it, you're going to have to lay a claim on it."

What a peculiar thing for Marcie to say. Did he want it? He never thought of the ranch that way, wanting it. Inheriting it, owning it, selling it or not selling it—such thoughts had been on his mind for years, even as he and his younger brother, Mark, circled each other on the subject, Mark, the real-estate developer, telling him that Montana was the last best place, by which he meant a developer's dream, and Hall saying such speculations were stupid, that their mother would never go along with one of his schemes. So what might Marcie think it meant, him wanting the ranch? To do what with it?

But still, he knew it was outrageous, probably morally bankrupt as well, for him to simply sit back at his desk, upon his mother's death. It was the sort of thing Mark would do, was almost certainly doing at this very second in Denver.

"Okay," he said. "You're right." He thanked her and told her he loved her. "We'll drive," he added, taking pleasure at least from the image of them working across the country in his new Toyota. Maybe it would snow on the way.

It was cold that stalked them across the country, dry and clear cold through New York and Ohio and across the Northern Plains, making their gas fill-ups and meals and arrivals at motels into frigid dashes across hostile tarmac. From visit to visit to the Plains, Hal always forgot what

Canadian cold was like, not the "Montreal Express" that Boston-area weatherpeople liked to prattle about, but the real thing, full of colors that had crystallized in the wind. That was what real cold was, something the cattle could see, a kind of recognition one could find in the black ice of their eyes in the morning. In Massachusetts, people liked to talk about the temperature as if it were a contest; on the Plains, the cold was private information, like love.

It was getting dark outside when they finally pulled into the ranch yard, but the house was ablaze with lights. He'd been struck by that astonishing sight from three miles away, the house on its rise below a backdrop of higher ridges, looking like a cruise ship taking people on an Arctic adventure through the ice floes. The closer they got, the more this sight alarmed him; perhaps something had happened in the house and strangers, or the police, had been searching every corner. He could not imagine Roy living like this, as if he were celebrating release from Jean's frugal ways; for as long as Hal had known Roy—and especially after he had married Jean and moved in—Hal had pictured him in his own dusk, sitting happily under the dim tea-colored wash of a forty-watt bulb.

Hal turned off the car engine and sat for a moment or two trying to make sense of this sight. "That's strange as hell," he said, his heart pounding, but Marcie already knew it, and she had unbuckled, flicked the handle, and stepped out in a single motion. Hal caught up to her on the shoveled path, and he leaned into the back door to give it the extra shoulder it always needed to break the seal of the weather stripping, but it did not open and he bounced painfully.

"Jesus!" he said through the howl of the wind, rubbing his bicep. "It's locked." They looked at each other while he gave the knob a few more twists to be sure that this unprecedented thing was really happening.

Hal pounded and searched out the doorbell, which he wasn't at all sure worked. The back door gave into a boot-room, and then through another door into the kitchen, and God knew what it would take to get Roy's attention.

"You told him we were coming. Right?" said Marcie.

"Of course I did. But I couldn't tell him exactly when." He kicked the door, hard enough to hurt his frozen toes, and was getting ready to jump into the waist-deep snow in search of an unlocked window when they heard movement.

Shannon Avery came to the door with a shotgun, raised, the side-by-side muzzles fixed on him like an owl's glinty gaze.

"Jesus," yelled Hal.

Shannon was big, that's how he remembered her, one of those large women who would have been powerful men but instead had to contend with too much hip, too much thigh. Her face was heavy and broad too, though there was nothing soft about those full cheeks, and especially not at this moment, because not only was she clearly surprised and very frightened to be confronting someone beating on the door almost hard enough to break it down, she was damn ready to put up a fight.

"Hal," she said. "God help me, I couldn't guess."

"What is going on?" said Hal.

She lowered the gun and backed away from the door, letting them in. "No one told me you were coming." She was still trembling.

Hal had so many questions and protests in his mind that he could only find the words to give voice to the simplest one. "Why the hell are all these lights on?"

"I'm here alone," she answered. She was a town girl; she'd been raised, like all town girls, to hear the extra dangers lurking up here in the high ranchlands. In the old days, people froze to death on the way to or from the ranches, were found in the spring still clutching their grocery lists or the gifts they planned to give their sweethearts.

"Where's Roy?" They had made their way into the kitchen, painfully bright, fixtures that as far as Hal could remember, had never been used. No wonder Roy was not sitting at the table with his cup of coffee, as he would surely have been if anything about this moment were normal; he would have been blinded. He was probably hiding under a blanket in the bedroom.

"He's out—"

Hal interrupted. "Then what are you doing here?"

"I'm looking after things," she said, and even at the height of his confusion, he knew what she said was reasonable by almost any standard, except those unmeetable standards one holds for home, the seat of one's memory. No one—especially not her—could be expected to understand why all these lights and a locked door seemed so sinister to him.

"I guess. Sure," said Hal, relenting most of the way.

"Why are you treating me like this," Shannon asked.

"I just didn't expect you to be here."

"I've got my own life to look after, you before"

Hal looked around at the kitchen, the dishes and remains of a steak dinner still scattered on the counter, complete with an open bottle of red Bordeaux from, he had no doubt, his father's long-untouched cellar. She didn't seem to have been depriving herself; she wasn't acting like a person making a sacrifice. Still, he began to feel that he had overreacted badly, and he apologized for it.

"Somebody has to keep an eye on things. Jean was very particular. This was what she planned."

Planned? In the few seconds of silence, he tried to recall exactly what Roy had said about what had killed his mother. A heart attack, never woke up. He'd made it sound sudden as a knife, but it wasn't; Hal could easily have guessed that, he just hadn't thought it through until now. She hadn't simply died; she had been dying, making plans, inviting all sorts of people, people she could pay and be done with to help her tidy up her affairs, to help her get this last chore done. But not him. Hal walked over to the window at the end of the kitchen, looked out across the frozen haylands across to the mountains, through the moon, through the wind, through the years. His mother had loved this view, and as a young bride from Philadelphia had made his father construct a window seat here for her, as if she might curl up at her leisure and compose short lyrics, the Emily Dickinson of the West. The seat had long ago become a place for mail and magazines, for small bits of broken machinery, stripped bolts, shattered castings.

"She had been quite ill since Christmas," Shannon said, and she didn't try to pretend that this wasn't news to Hal; she'd been the one who had propped Jean up to make her last few evasive phone calls to her sons, twice or three times a month. *We're getting on real good,* she would say, her Bryn Mawr accent and speech long gone. *Don't come out this winter; I don't want to heat the upstairs.*

Hal thanked her, because she was offering to fill in the blanks for him, but didn't want to hear any more. "Where is Roy, anyway?" he asked.

At this, Shannon looked uncomfortable again, as if he were going to resume attacking her. In answer to the question, she pointed out the picture window into the ranch yard. "It wasn't my idea," she protested.

It took him a second or two to understand what she was

talking about: the bunkhouse. There were lights on in the bunkhouse. "Oh, Roy," he said. "What in God's name are you doing out there?"

The bunkhouse hadn't been used in years; they didn't hire a hay crew anymore, now that they made round bales, just a teenager or two from town. As a child, Hal had been afraid of the place. His father was a hard man, a brutal boss, and Hal didn't want to hear the crew plotting mutiny, ten against one. He worried that if he walked too close to the door one of them might come out and snatch him. Even as an adult, Hal was repelled by the thought of that deserted shell, still dank with the alcohol-soaked sweat of all those men, a fetid pile of mattresses in one corner; even the light, through the small windows, seemed polluted and yellow like tobacco juice. How could Roy move over there, in the cold, at his age, after all that he had done to retrieve himself from that life?

Roy opened the door as Hal approached through the wind. Behind his small and tense body the stovepipe was cherry red and the heat blew past Hal as he entered. The scene inside was not as bad as he had remembered; Roy had brought over a Morris chair from the television room and a few floor lamps. He had a good radio, a Bose, that was picking up some sort of talk show from the CBC. The building was L-shaped, and he had closed the door to the larger back wing, making an almost cozy space. All it needed was a rug to cover a floor that was brown with the damage of ranch hands, their boot heels, their knives, their drunken rages. Roy was wearing the blue jeans and sweatshirt he always wore, but had on a pair of bright blue polarfleece slippers that could only have been a present from Jean; they made a scuffing sound as he walked, like a child in Dr. Denton's. He had been reading the paper, and his half-moon reading glasses were folded over the crossword puzzle.

"Roy," Hal blurted. "Why are you here?"

Roy looked at him blankly. He didn't answer. Hal realized in a sickening flood that Roy might have thought Hal was asking why he was on the ranch at all, and not gone, back to Great Falls, back to California, now that his protector was dead.

"I mean," said Hal quickly, "why in the bunkhouse? You didn't tell me you'd come over here. Why aren't you living in the house?"

Again Roy hesitated before he answered. Hal reminded himself that these pauses did not mean that Roy was strategizing his responses, but were simply the way he conversed. He always planned exactly what he was going to say before he said it, and even if his sentences were short, they were always complete. Hal had never heard Roy use an "um" or a "you know" or a stammer to buy time, which Hal himself did frequently.

"I got all I need," he said, and he waved his hand to invite Hal to take a second look at his new home, to appreciate the easy chair, the bed made tight as a board with a cheerful red bedspread, the lamps, the gas range and refrigerator installed in the last year or two of the old regime. The pot of coffee on the stove, mixing its scent with the woodsmoke, made the place smell as comforting as a Christmas shop. Roy seemed to be asking Hal why any man would be dissatisfied with such a simple and comfortable home, and Hal could only recognize that this was no temporary accommodation but a permanent move for Roy; this is where he wanted to be at the end, and not in the ranch house. Throughout his marriage to Jean, he'd never called the ranch house home; it was "Jean's place," or the "owner's house," or just, "the ranch house": a function, a purpose, a reason for being.

"Okay. You're the boss." Was this tiny little choice, this preference to return to what he had known for most of his life, what he might have wanted Hal not to see?

"I'm sorry, Roy, about Mom. For you. I really am."

Roy had been holding himself terse and guarded so far, but when Hal said that, he let his small bony frame slump and tears formed in his eyes. "Oh, she was a good old girl."

"You were happy together."

Roy looked up at Hal's eyes to ensure that Hal would never overlook that one all-important fact. "We were," Roy said, and there was still surprise in it for him, seven years later, still wonder at his fortune. What a powerful kind of love it is, thought Hal, that forever elicits disbelief.

Roy sat back into his Morris chair, and Hal pulled a stool to join him at the fire.

"Do you have everything you want?" Hal asked. "Are there things you want me to do?"

"Shannon's been a good bit of help to us. Since Jean took ill."

With Roy, as with Shannon, he did not need to pretend that he had been getting daily bulletins from her doctor; Roy would know that to the end she had been giving orders to keep her decline, her pain, her needs, from her sons. "I never even knew she was sick," he said.

Roy could do nothing but give a sympathetic shrug.

"Was it bad for her? For you?"

"No," he said, a burr again in his voice. "Just slow. She felt tired, mostly."

Hal looked Roy straight in the eyes. "I know you didn't want me to come out. But Marcies's with me," he added, as a consolation.

Roy had always been sweet on Marcie, and at the mention of her name his face brightened. "So she come out with you," he stated mostly to himself.

"Yes," said Hal.

Roy smiled; a private memory. Marcie had always flirted with Roy, teased him; it seemed that no one in Roy's life—certainly not Jean—had ever poked fun at him, a luxury to be enjoyed by people with more money or fewer faults.

Hal waited while this memory ran its course, and Roy began to speak again in his jerky monotone. "I'm glad you come out, Hal. That was Jean talking, saying not to. I'm glad you're here. We need you, is the thing."

Hal stood up. It was time to call it a day. He'd woken up that morning in Rapid City, South Dakota, and he was tired. Roy was tired, and Roy was also a good person, someone Hal had come to admire even though each visit always seemed to begin with the same scratchiness as this one, the same wary circling that began almost fifty years ago, when Hal was four and Roy came off the road looking for work, a hungry and lonely teenager, and got his first job here because Hal's mother took pity on him. And why not? By pitying Roy she was taking pity on herself—something she would never allow herself to do otherwise—in a marriage that had so quickly turned loveless, leaving a young Eastern bride alone and miserable. What Jean had done was the essence of ranch life, mingling intimately with others who had lived so differently. Hal's father had often warned him about these hay hands, how little anyone really knew about them, but still, as restless teenagers Hal and his brother had looked forward to the arrival of the hay crews in those long, solitary summers, and had become better persons because of the truths these men had brought with them, truths about keeping your dignity when you have nothing but a pair of jeans to your name; finding your joys wherever they might be hiding, in a bottle, a night's lover, a memory; trusting nothing and no one but the hours, which have done right enough by you thus far.

"Well?" said Marcie. She was thawing some steaks for them in the microwave. She had poured herself some of the remainder of Shannon's Bordeaux. She was cheerful, bustling through this kitchen, and Hal was more than grateful that they seemed to be alone. He jerked his head to one side, asking where Shannon was.

"She went to bed. She's in your old room."

"I'm not sleeping in Mom's room," said Hal; it was the only other room in the house with two beds.

"No. I didn't think you would. Me neither."

Hal walked over to the liquor cabinet, expecting it to offer nothing but cooking sherry and crusty thirty-year-old leftover crème de menthe, but there was a nice full bottle of Jack Daniel's there, and he snatched it at the neck. "Maybe I'm just going to get drunk," he said.

"How's Roy?"

"It's very sweet. He's moved in, he has everything he needs."

"He's the one person around here who knows what he wants."

"He always has been." Hal let a little bourbon trickle down his throat; it felt good; it reminded him of his father in a way that was surprisingly pleasant. What he really wanted to do was to enjoy his liquor, have dinner, and then head on up to his brother's old single bed, and make love.

Marcie went over to the stove and pulled open the broiler with a loud squeaking of a faulty hinge. She went off into the mudroom—also a freezer room, junk room, kitchen storeroom—and came back with the broiler pan, shiny with grease. "Gross," she said. "She really let this place get disgusting, you know."

"That was just her way of telling everyone to screw off."

Marcie didn't debate the point. She slapped the steak on the pan, and was about to slide it into the stove when she said, "Jean's here, you know."

"No kidding. She's already haunting the place."

"I mean her ashes are here. In the den. Go look while I get dinner ready."

He paused to pour a little more bourbon into his glass and then walked into the den. It was his favorite room in the house in winter, with its fireplace, its slightly battered upholstery, its bookshelves, and its small windows to the north. In summer the den was too dark, and reminded everyone in the family that the spring in Montana came late and suddenly, without the gradual warming and blossoming of New England, and that the fall—though a kinder season—was never far away. Marcie had lit a fire and on a side table, a Chippendale that Jean had brought with her so many years ago when she left Philadelphia as a young bride, Marcie had placed the urn. She had lit candles on either side.

The urn, a copper color, stood mute and straight as a

fence post. That was right: Jean had lived as someone who prevailed. Her power had been endurance, like the women who came West only a generation earlier, and though they put lace—if they could find it—around the windows of their cabins, and though they made bonnets from fabrics that favored their coloring and taught their daughters family quilt patterns even as those same girls were learning how to butcher a hog or bury a father, though they tried to keep what could be lovely about their womanhood alive, there wasn't much time or place for it. Hal's mother was hard because she had to be; maybe that thought was the beginning of forgiveness. He'd married someone as unlike her as he could, as frivolous and unpolitical and undisciplined a girl as any college student could possibly have been in those days, the sixties. Marcie had changed, though Jean had not—not with Hal anyway, whom she'd protected as a soft boy and then cast out as one who didn't have the stuff it took to run a ranch, take a man's place. That was all fine, really it was. For the best, at least for a good many years. But in the end, she said nothing. She died as she had lived, wrapped in the deceptions that kept her whole. She had no good-byes to make, no last pieces of wisdom. Breathtakingly complete it was, her death: a pot of ash, tidy as it could get; nothing for Hal, or Mark, to remember, nothing to mourn.

Hal and Marcie started the night out together, side by side like teenagers, in Mark's childhood bed, but as usual Hal woke in the stillest hour and could not get back to sleep. The house was cold—it was perhaps twenty below outside now, though the wind appeared to have died down—and he found a slightly smelly sweatsuit in Mark's closet. He came downstairs and made himself some tea, and sat at the kitchen table. The porch light was still on at the bunkhouse; the yard light over the equipment sheds was casting its bronze glow; and down by the wintering barns, he could see the cold shapes of the cattle clustered out of the weather. The cattle knew that there was storm coming, falling into the sudden slack in the wind, and over their heads, above the ridgepole of the barns, Hal could see the slight orange tint of a chancy dawn. Life would be easier for him if he hated what he saw. They could have this operation wrapped up by fall; they could have the herd sold, equipment auctioned, Roy set up in a small house of his own in town, Mark's bulldozers scraping off the pitiful little band of soil and leaving the place exposed for what it truly was: a piece of rock. A hard and unloving place. A place that had taken both his parents and wrung out of them whatever was soft or kind or even simply human. A place that Hal had tried for nearly forty years to remove from his heart because what did it matter, a ranch, this one in particular? How to comass this primordial pull back to a home place when the place itself seemed to have so little room or love?

He was still in this dark mood when Shannon came down at six, lugging a heavy suitcase. He'd been arrogant and suspicious of her last night, truly unforgivable, if he recollected right, and he was glad that he might have a chance to do better now. "You're going?" he asked.

"You're here now." Yes, she was still angry.

He stood up and began to make his way to the kitchen. "You can't go out without some breakfast." He was almost surprised when she nodded and sat. She was maybe ten years younger than Hal—he'd known her oldest brother, Frederick, when they were growing up, and at least two of her sisters. As far as Hal knew, they were all gone now, gone from this valley. Shannon probably had a couple or more children of her own now, in their twenties, and a husband who worked for the county. She'd come into this house for pay but sat here now as something more than an employee. She knew the secrets of this place, just as Roy had known them, had remembered them for all those years before returning for good.

Hal got the coffee going and then began to scramble some eggs. He did not ask Shannon what she wanted—she would take what she got; people needed breakfast out here. He made toast and brought it all over to the table when it was done, a small feast. He'd made amends.

She thanked him and began to eat. Outside Hal heard the squeal of Roy's storm door across the night's wind-blown ice crystals, and they watched as his form, dark in its winter covering, marked only by the puffs of brilliant white breath, walked across the yard and down to the barns.

"How long can Roy do this?" asked Hal.

"Long as it takes," she answered. "It'd kill him to stop, you know that."

Hal did; anyone could know that about Roy. "I'm not here to kick him out. Is that what people think?"

"Well, people don't know about you two boys, do they."

"I guess not. More coffee?" he asked, pot held high. It was Maxwell House, but coffee was like blood on these ranches, warmth and even, in the few lingering moments of every meal, an occasion for fellowship. Shannon raised her cup to the pot.

"So what do people think?"

"Oh."

"Come on, Shannon."

"Two rich boys, I guess. Don't trust Mark. Hal, well, not much ranch in that boy." Shannon took no pleasure in passing this along, and none of it surprised Hal in the least.

"So they think we'll be selling out just as soon as we can get our hands on the place?"

"Something like that. It's happening all over the valley, you know." She got up to take the plates over to the sink. She'd be off in a few minutes, back into town, maybe over-joyed at being set free, maybe angry that Hal and Marcie had come to destroy her deal, which seemed, as far as Hal could tell, to be completely open-ended. He didn't fault her, one way or the other.

"So what about my mother?" he asked.

"What about her?"

"What did she think I was going to do? What did she want? What the hell did she want to happen here?"

Shannon was standing at the door now, pulling on her mittens. "I can't answer that, Hal. You can't ask me. Talk to Sam Bicknell," she said—his parents' lawyer. She almost let that go as her final line, but reappeared around the mudroom doorway. "You may think I heard a lot of things from Jean during those last weeks, but I didn't. If you think I know anything, I don't. If she had plans on her mind, she took them with her, as far as I know. I can't imagine what she was like as a mother, but if it makes you feel better, she didn't treat anyone else much better. No one but Roy."

At ten, after Marcie came down, cold, somewhat bad-tempered from an uncomfortable night, they went to town. Hal was pleased that his Toyota sprang to life; such were the few reliable satisfactions for him these days. The sky was overcast now, and darker to the north; snow for sure was on its way. But even in his beloved new toy, he drove inattentively, and was distracted enough to speed around the wide turn at the bottom of Millersburg's Main Street, the precise place where over the years he had gotten three speeding tickets. He deserved them; it was a blind curve that landed right in the heart of town, but that was back when Main Street bustled with people, and even in winter there were bound to be kids playing in the street, horses and cattle blocking the way, slow-moving tractors chugging up to Peltzer's Feed and Seed. This time, there was nothing to hit, just a few trucks nosed in at the café, and a broad treeless street laid out for a population that no longer existed.

They parked in front of the café, amid the trucks, and though the windows were clouded with the feathered iridescence of ice crystals, Hal could tell little inside had changed from his last visit. Over the years the number of people who recognized him in town had steadily diminished, like the population itself, and he and Marcie took a table in front of the stunned and suddenly silent gaze of people who wondered just who in the hell these people were and why the hell they had walked into this private spot. The man—Hal—was carrying a briefcase, yet. But there was always someone who spotted him, a rancher who knew his mother and father, or even a middle-aged waitress he'd once thought of trying to date, and this time it was the receptionist at the law firm, Bicknell and Bicknell.

"We're just heading over to your office," said Hal across the empty oilcloth-covered tables between them. He held up his briefcase.

"Too bad about Jean," said one of the older men.

Hal thanked him, and the rest of the group, as they nodded along. "How's the cattle business?" he asked.

Someone whistled, a coarse and not very informative response, as if they wondered why this Easterner would care. "Sixty cents," said one of the men finally.

Hal knew what he meant, the most recent auction price, but it had been a long time since he saw his mother's books, and whether this was just another in a long line of rancher's complaints or a real change in the beef business, he didn't know. Still, he tried to answer back knowledgeably. "Hard to make a buck," he said.

"Oh, hell," said one man who Hal suspected was a Rangley, a family that didn't like his father. "Shannon and Roy don't have to worry about Dunning Creek Ranch paying its bills with cattle ranching."

Marcie clamped her hand on Hal's forearm, and her fingers tightened into the clenched sinews. They had drunk their coffee and paid for it, and she kept her hand on his arm until she had tugged him back out onto the street.

"It's not as if no one knows your family had money," said Marcie. Hal angrily zipped up his parka and they turned for the lawyer's office. "People must have been making cracks like that since the day your father arrived here, sixty years ago."

Hal could think of nothing to add—what Marcie said was true enough. They reached Bicknell and Bicknell—the only freshly painted storefront on the street—in silence. There was a Mercedes out front; just because ranching was in trouble, it didn't mean the lawyers had to suffer.

They took their seats in the small windowless conference

room, and Hal was relieved that it was the elder Bicknell, one of his father's few good friends, who came in with several thick file folders under his arm. He was wearing a white Western shirt and a bola tie and ostrich boots: a real Montana man from a family that first came to the Plains on the promises of a flyer from the Northern Pacific Railroad during the teens, and instead of quitting when the freeze and drought returned in the twenties, the family had simply kept going west, across the Divide, and landed in this verdant and sheltered valley. Sam Bicknell, who must have been almost ninety, had lived through it all.

He greeted Hal and Marcie warmly, and for an hour or so went through the details of the will, which Hal had never read, had never asked to read. Oh, the place was coming to Hal and Mark, to do whatever their brotherly rivalry could devise, but not before Roy died. Not before he had lived out his life, protected from every assault, every attempt by unscrupulous heirs to pry him loose, every nefarious strategy to shunt him aside. Shannon was in the mix as well, as agent and manager, bookkeeper and protector. There was only one way to interpret these last words from the grave: A woman who had seemed to trust so few people in her life, had, in death, mistrusted most of all her own sons.

When Sam was done, Hal sat there in this office, clock ticking, a phone ringing in the next office and the receptionist saying "I almost died." Marcie put her hand on his arm, this time in support: You're not the person that your mother has described, she was saying. Hal leaned back in his chair. Above Sam there were a few musty photographs from many years ago, ranching scenes, cattle being driven along the state road, Millersburg as a boomtown with solid lines of black Fords up both sides of Main Street. He brought a hand to his lower lip and pinched it. No one spoke for a moment. "In other words," he said finally, "my mother didn't trust Mark and me to do the right thing."

"I wouldn't put it just like that."

"Then how would you put it?"

"She wanted to relieve you of the responsibilities."

"No," said Hal. "Relieving us of responsibilities would be the last thing on her list. If my mother had to choose one of her sons to enact her wishes, or a virtual stranger, she'd pick the stranger, someone like Shannon. She knew she was dying, and she chose to speak her last words to a kitchen girl she used to refer to as 'the blob.' "

Again, no one spoke, because Sam knew it was the truth; Hal could imagine well his conversations with Jean in this office over the years, and could imagine that Sam might often have put forward her sons as the appropriate people to take care of this or that, to give her aid. Hal could imagine the sudden, almost furious flash of impatience in her eyes as Sam made these gentle recommendations, the way she must have turned steely and dangerous, as if she'd take the family business and walk. Even if understood and partially forgiven, they could still hurt, these imagined memories, they hurt like hell.

"It's okay," said Hal. "This is nothing new."

Marcie knew well to leave Hal alone—they had ridden out from town without a single word—and he was grateful, as grateful as a man could be watching the last trace of an illusion about his family drain out of his life. He made himself a sandwich, tuna fish that tasted dry as feathers, but she left him in peace.

He pulled on his parka and stepped outside. In the sky there were black grains of air in the north: heavy snow really was coming, not just this dusting. That was just one more thing about Montana that he had forgotten: that you can see weather coming from days away. The chill was calmer now; the wind had stopped and the light on the buildings of the ranch, this small assemblage of utilitarian structures, magnified the textures of their siding, the steep shine of their metal roofs. Those sharp peaks and low eaves had stood this way for season after season, a couple of them almost from the first years that this land was claimed by people who thought they had the right to it, the right to call a place home. Beyond these structures, across the valley, he could see the partitioning of haylands in the expanses of snow as smooth on the surface as the clipped soil four feet below. Take the history—take the *baggage*, as Marcie had said—out of it, and the ranch was just a house or two, a few buildings, six hundred acres of land owned and another three thousand leased from the government. It was a business, a place to make a life; it had its seductions, in the brilliant heat of July high noons, in the silent cold of a day like this, when all is expectation, when nothing breathes a word.

The cattle in the sheds did not take fright as he approached. They stood squeezed against each other's round sides, with only an occasional head forced out of the pack by the jostling and compression of the herd, their backs making a thick blanket of hot veldt. He leaned over the fence, forearms resting on the top rail and hands clasped in front: the classic rancher's pose, but what did Hal know of these whitefaced beasts? Sixty cents a pound. He couldn't remember what a good one was supposed to weigh, what the diseases were that could ruin a rancher if he didn't spot them early, what combination of cruelty and patience made them file so meekly into the last cattle cars on their way to the slaughterhouses. He picked out one, head forced low against the fence rails, and he stared at her through the deep mysteries of her eyes; he reached through to feel the coarse forelock that tufted like a spiny weed from between her rounded horn bumps. The hair was grainy; stretched tight, it would sing like a violin string.

He left the cattle and stepped into the equipment sheds. So many hundreds of thousands of dollars of steel and rubber, hose and wire. These giant articulated green monsters were nothing like those playful little Fords and Farmalls of his youth; pop the sheet metal off one of those and there the whole thing would be, an engine and a drive train almost as visible as one of those clear plastic models, with tiny blue pistons going gaily up and down as you turned the little handle, and your father was there saying *See, that's the compression stroke, see the valves shut, see the shaft turn?* Your father maybe, but not Hal's. Hal could see him now, at the far end of this shed, in the shop, working at the bench, taciturn, anger covering up his own mistakes. There had been little his father taught Hal about these things, and less yet that Hal had learned about them. A rancher couldn't survive without these skills, the skills it took to repair a baler out there under the sun, every hour lost a disaster.

He went last into the horse barns, just three horses now. Nothing too great either; that's one thing Hal hadn't forgotten, how to spot a good horse. These creatures, he knew their desires and their complaints like his own telephone number. It had always amused him, encountering horsey people back East, to listen to the absolute crap they propounded about these dumb beasts. His ideas about them were all Western: break them of their will, force them to yours, as simple as that. But oh, when all was done, was there any pleasure he had ever known that equaled the feeling of his body landing in the saddle, and then heading out into the blue morning for a day's work, his work and the horse's work? No. No stirring of a gladness and anticipation for the hours ahead that was so simple and so cleansing, so utterly and completely worth it. And yes, seated on that high perch he could reach down below the mane and put a hand on a foamy and salty wither and say "Good horse, I mean you no harm." That joy was here, on this ranch. That pleasure and a lot of others: this bony aromatic landscape; the clean shave of a mower cutting its sheer swath through a tangled field of alfalfa; the smell of a hot lunch calling him in from the sheds at midday; the explosion of joy that could attend a simple Hershey bar when one hadn't set foot off the ranch for two weeks; a stop at a Dairy Queen on the way to Butte; the cold pitiless nights during calving—soon upon them—ending with the slick fur of the newborn calf; the moment at day's end when the farmer or the rancher can stand in the middle of the yard and know that however little it may seem he had accomplished, it was enough. These small moments would not have sustained him in his twenties, so eager for the praise of others; or in his thirties, so busy with his own skills; or in his forties, so restless and quick to reject. But now, yes, now, these were once again the things he loved, dreams hovering for so long just out of his reach.

His brother, Mark, was right. This particular valley, and their little town with its once-proud granite Grange Hall and lines of empty storewindows that had once been filled with such delights: Matchbox cars and saddlery and flower-print dresses and the silver shine of gifts, bowls and belt buckles—this was one of the most beautiful places either Mark or Hal had ever seen. They'd neither of them forgotten that for one second; anyone knowing about it would gladly pay money to visit there. What that meant to Mark was that the first person who bought up the main street and hired the architect and wrote a brochure, and built a golf course and ran a chairlift up Eagle Ridge to the Lookout, that person, and that person's brother, would make a bloody fortune.

Roy had been asleep in his Morris chair when Hal knocked and then walked in. He greeted Hal in a voice a little above a whisper.

"Hey," said Hal. "How you doing?"

"Just a little tired, is all. I can still do a good day's work, come spring."

"Roy, you don't have to do a day's work. For all intents and purposes, you own this place. You're not a ranch hand."

This was no comfort to Roy, Hal knew that; however Hal might want to couch it, this would sound to Roy as if he was getting a gold watch he didn't want. There was wariness, even terror, in Roy's eyes, and Hal knew that even to this moment's heartbeat, this was exactly what his mother had tried to avoid. From the far side of her recent death, he could hear her howling with frustration and rage.

"I know why you didn't want me to come out here. You

were worried that I'd wreck everything you and Mom had set up."

"It wasn't me," answered Roy, speaking only for himself. "I already told you that."

"What a shit she must have thought I am."

Roy seemed to understand that most of this was a conversation Hal could have only with himself. But he said, "You come out, didn't you? Didn't take much to keep Mark back in Denver."

"I wouldn't have come either unless Marcie had stepped in."

Roy shrugged; as far as he was concerned, there was little difference between what Hal did on his own and what Marcie persuaded him to do. Roy pointed to the stool in the corner, and began to get up in order to pull it over for Hal. Hal reached out, put his hand on Roy's thin arm to stop him, and grabbed the stool himself.

"I guess I came out because I figured I'd be needed, even though you said everything was taken care of. Fact is, everything *is* taken care of, right? You and Shannon, you've got what you need for now."

Roy nodded; he had nothing to add.

"So I guess we'll just stick around for a couple of days, through this storm maybe." Hal pictured his office at the bank, a sterile place, decorated with framed tombstones of deals he'd been involved in, a print of old Boston the decorator had decreed, his few pictures of Marcie and the girls. His heart fell.

"What's wrong, Hal?"

"I feel as if I've been thrown off the ranch for the second time. This time for good."

"Not by me, you ain't."

"No. Not by you. By her."

Roy took a long time to speak again. When he started up, he was precise with his words, as always. "If you're coming back out here to settle a score with her, I'll fight you. Indeed I will."

Yes, Hal admitted to himself, that might have been part of the reason he had come out, as of a few days ago. But there was nothing left to settle: the dry ink on a lawyer's paper—that was all the settling anyone needed to do.

"Hal, your family was a strange breed. I give no credit to your dad, and you know that. I loved my wife, but I wouldn't have wanted to be her son. No way." He whistled, as if the total of all his tough life wouldn't equal that fate.

"Jean had her ways. I tried to make her call you at the end, and she almost did. It's just that habit gets harder and harder to break as life goes on. I'm sorry she didn't, for your sake, but hers was the bigger loss."

"Yes. I think it was."

"I can't explain her to you. I can't tell you anything you don't know. There's nothing more to learn."

"I understand."

Roy leaned forward in his chair. Hal could see the arthritic pains as they shot through his eyes. "It's time to let her rest in peace. She's mine to grieve now. Let me do it."

"Okay."

Roy picked up his hand and pointed a long, scaly finger at Hal. "You got nothing to prove to her, or to your dad, anymore. That's done. Do you understand me?"

Hal had never seen Roy like this, pointing at him, grilling him. Roy sat back, puffing slightly from this effort. Hal got up, walked over to the woodstove, and threw a few logs in. The air was white outside; the snow was on them now.

"Then what now?" asked Hal, still standing at the stove.

"Well, I don't have no say."

"I'm asking you for your say. Your say means everything to me." Hal's nose and his sinuses were suddenly blocked with tears, rushing to his eyes; his voice showed it, and Roy, who had been looking away in fear, perhaps, or in embarrassment, glanced up with a start. "I'm asking you to tell me what to do."

"You got a good life back East, Hal."

"I don't. My career may be going down the tubes."

"Then stay here."

"And do what?"

"Run the ranch."

"I don't know anything about ranching, you know that. Besides, that's what my mother was trying to prevent."

"I told you. Your mother's dead. You been waiting for

this to happen and now it has. You don't have to pretend that ain't so with me. She's dead, and it's time for you to come on home."

In the afternoon, Hal and Marcie cooked a turkey, peeled potatoes, dug out a jar of corn put up by Jean just a few months ago. The snow had started to white out the sky, the mountains, the distant pines. By morning, his Toyota would be buried and immobile, four-wheel drive or not. The flakes, one by one, would cover the last surface Jean had looked at, and when it all melted in spring, the land would be new.

They baked biscuits—a little flat and burned—and, just to test themselves, just to remind themselves where they had come from, they baked a Boston cream pie, Hal doing the cake, Marcie the custard. They did this side by side, passing canisters and implements back and forth like team members. With the cooking done, and with the peace of this house now theirs to make and enjoy alone, and with the calming snow showing white against the windows, Hal led Marcie into the living room in front of the fire and cajoled her out of her sweatsuit.

Later, at six sharp, they heard the footsteps through the snow. Marcie went to the door, and from around the corner Hal could hear the sounds of his wife hugging Roy; he could feel her unabashed joy at greeting him, telling him Come in, take off that coat, leave your boots. He'd brought his slippers and soon he scuffed around the corner, into Hal's view.

He went right to the table, as he had always done in the old days, and sat right down. Hal sat in his father's chair, and Marcie began to pass the platters and bowls. There was little talk as they ate; it was a custom of the house in his father's day, never a word at the table until the coffee was served. Roy ate hungrily, a huge meal for someone so old and so thin. When he finished, he pushed back his plate, pulled in his coffee cup, and waited for someone to speak.

"So what do you think, Roy?" asked Marcie. "Would we be crazy to try this?"

"It's a good life. There's room for mistakes. I'm here to testify to that. There's mercies all through it."

Mercies, thought Hal. Marcie would love the theology in that word: What happened to them was being guided by a God who would show mercy to those who deserved it. She and Roy had always seemed to share this belief, the same belief whether it came from the gilded pulpit of St. Paul's Church in Newton, Massachusetts, or from the words of other redeemed souls around a table at an AA meeting. Hal had never come to that belief, and he might never. But Hal understood mercy when it was being offered to him, and he understood his blessings: a wife who stood beside him, two daughters to care for, a man to guide him, a place to come home to.

It was one week ago tonight that Jean lay dying in this house, upstairs in her bedroom, surrounded by the things she cherished: her books, her photographs, the odd bits of linen and china that she had brought out here as a young bride. This was all she needed to accompany her from this world to the next. Hal could give these things to her and not ask for any more in return, which was lucky. He pictured her struggling for breath, and then the look of fear that must have been there when the final breath would not come. It was Roy that she saw last, the one real love of her life.

The Late Night News

*I*n one of those big ancestral arks along one of those Chesapeake Bay rivers, Martin Grey walked into the kitchen to pour himself another scotch. Behind him, the television blared out a newsmagazine show; when his son Albert had called a few minutes earlier, Martin said he was watching a "mazagine" show, after Albert's childhood malaprop. Once they had hung up, this reference had left a melancholy flavor in the air. Martin was nearly sixty, a tall man, undeniably bald but still fairly fit, through no real effort of his own. He was wearing a tattered blue terry-cloth bathrobe over his white shirt and flannel trousers, and he had one sock off. One can dress in that comfortable manner when one is living alone, and he had been living at Waterford alone since his second wife, Amy, moved back to New York, several months ago.

The main house, dark and empty, awaited him through

a swinging door; lately he had been sleeping on the fold-out couch in the farm office just off the kitchen; if there had been a shower in the lavatory, he'd have gone for days without leaving the servants' wing. Ever since Amy left he had been thinking that he should buy or rent a condo somewhere, with a spare bedroom for visits from the kids, but he had no idea what to do with Waterford. You don't rent out a place like that; more likely, you hire someone to live there—if you're lucky, you can find a couple, a retired county worker and his wife. And you don't sell a place like that, not after you fought bitterly with your uncle for years to retain it in the family, intact, as if you had an obligation to the State of Maryland or the National Archives, or some agency somewhere that held families accountable for preserving their heirlooms.

Martin clanked a few ice cubes into his glass and poured himself a solid slug of scotch. He was not a drunk, not like a good many of his friends and neighbors, Betty Chester, both the Manfreds, Judge—oh God, yes—Judge Barton. But what he had just poured himself was not exactly a cocktail, not at eleven at night, a good belt of undiluted whisky. Perhaps he could claim that it was to help him sleep, but still, this was drinking with a purpose and it had been going on for too long, since Amy left, which was long enough to get him into trouble. He glanced down at the liquid he was bringing to his lips, a thick caramel in color and smoky as a brushfire. He told himself he didn't want to end up barfing all over his couch, but he took a sip anyway.

The wind was blowing outside, whistling slightly through the interlace of bare beech boughs at the windows, and from somewhere on the property he could hear a door, a shed door probably, thudding freely. Martin considered heading out to secure it. It was March, and already the winds that blew up the Bay were warmer than the air; soon he would be leaving the windows open against the mold that each winter seemed to take over the house, seeping up through the concrete floor of the back rooms, a living substance in the wallpaper paste, a damp hang of rot in the attic. Summer was coming, and summer had always been good to him.

Amy and he had parted with the agreement that their four years together had been perfectly pleasant, but more than pleasant would have been needed to induce her to continue with her bifurcated life. When they met, on the ski slopes of Stratton, she was a fund-raising consultant living on the Upper West Side, and she had continued to commute to New York to work three or four days a week all through their marriage. Martin's life was unmovable: He was a country gentleman-slash-unlikely owner of a string of quite successful "Only Stop" convenience stores and gas stations. His territory was something locally known as the Delmarva Peninsula—those portions of three states floating uncertainly between the Chesapeake

Bay and the Atlantic Ocean. On the way down the aisle on their wedding day in a Vermont country inn—Amy was dressed in a slinky satin dress that so aroused Martin that he hardly listened to the proceedings—she had whispered, "This is madness," and she meant it as a statement of the power of whimsy in the face of poor odds. Martin had not thought of his marriage as madness, but maybe that was the problem: Maybe he had regarded their union too practically, people of roughly the same age, good in bed, an answer to the vague anxieties expressed by their children, his three and her four. There wasn't much whimsy in any of that.

As it turned out, their marriage was something that was easily undone: Amy had never given up her rent-controlled apartment on Riverside Drive. In the final few weeks before she left, she spoke of her waiting apartment—its clean uncased windows and doors, the bright parquet floor, a narrow kitchen filled with sturdy steel cabinetry—with the mounting joy of an exile finally permitted to return. Martin was hurt by this utter rejection of Waterford, of the Eastern Shore, the whole package of family and history this place embodied. Yet Martin could admit that she was not wrong to see leaving here after her short marriage as an escape, like the girls of generations past who believed they could escape Waterford into marriage. Martin probably should have gone with her, not that she had invited him.

He sat back down on his couch, searching out the remote control between the two cushions. He turned the TV off, grateful for the sudden silence, but continued to hold on to the remote, a solid and tangible link to the outside world. He ran the tip of his forefinger over the pleasingly cushioned plastic of the buttons like a man perusing a wine list.

Martin was at that age when much has been accumulated—and preserved, in his case—but so much still seems ungrasped and unsaid. It seemed his first marriage had blown by him like a fast freight. It had begun so young— Viv was a college junior—and was so immediately "blessed" with children that Martin felt he had lived one complete lifetime before he was forty. He recalled his years between marriages, which included his first entirely unplanned coinvestment in an Only Stop franchise, as an endless drive on the New Jersey Turnpike, up to Princeton to pick up or drop off the kids. Then his second marriage, and now this, drinking alone, drinking hard in a peculiarly WASP way— discreetly, at home, surrounded by cheerless antiques. His only satisfaction was the high quality of the scotch; his only comfort was the thought that he could do this forever if he wanted to or needed to.

Long ago Martin had learned that loneliness was like all other kinds of pain: endurable if you knew it would get no worse and if you could be certain that it would someday stop. Maybe that certainty was what his failure with Amy had finally taken away, leaving him with the feeling that he had made his last attempt at marriage and had failed twenty years short of the finish line. It could get a lot worse, this hollowness; he was just standing at the edge, looking into the pit, and it was a dangerous place to be, he knew that. The liquid voices were inviting him to jump in: You'll love it! You can't imagine how good permanent self-pity can feel! What else do you have on your calendar? One of these days, perhaps tonight, perhaps even this second, he would have to make a decision; his life was in his hands like a folded shadow; he was terrified of the dark.

Once again he heard that disquieting thumping from outside. There were always sounds in the air in this house, on this place: it was the reason so many people thought Waterford was haunted, but Martin had grown up with these thuds and creaks. As a child he had made his peace with the ghosts, deciding and then believing that they would come out only when he needed their help. This compact had meant that he did not need to imagine what form they might take, whether they would be ghastly with decay, or breezy, like smoke, or undistinguishable from a human, except perhaps for their clothing. His parents, who were somewhat old when they finally had their only child, bathed him in the kind of all-protective love that made faith possible. He remembered well that feeling, snug in his bed, but tonight this thumping out there was beginning to bother him. It seemed all too real. He could picture the screws on the door hinge backing out; the vision of this door, tomorrow morning, hanging cockeyed from a twisted lower hinge, did not please him, an all-too-perfect metaphor for his life. Yet he was too tired to go out there and attend to it now. He slid down in the couch enough to rest his head on the cushion, and made the beginning of a vow that come tomorrow, things were going to change.

Somewhere off in the house there was a loud noise. Martin sat up sharply; in fact, he had fallen asleep. He glanced at his watch. It was close to one o'clock; his glass, still half full, was wedged between his thighs. He listened for the thumping outside, but it had stopped, though the wind had not, and now there was this crash, or this shatter, or was it a duller noise, something whacking something? He held his breath while he listened; had there been any note of broken glass in the noise? It was most probably a tree branch, possibly a very large one indeed, broken off by the wind; it could have landed on the roof, brushed the house, even knocked through a window. But still, it was a real noise, enough to wake him up.

He stood to his feet a little too fast, and for a moment he skirted consciousness while his alcohol-thinned blood pumped into his brain. And then, there it was: another sound, which was neither crash nor shatter nor thud but the protesting cry of something being pried. A door. Martin could still not entirely believe it; was someone actually trying to break in Waterford's front door?

Panic rose through his throat. What should he do? Run

to the door and try to barricade it, get into a cartoonish pushing match with whatever it was outside? Grab the telephone? That was the problem with living out here; the state trooper was Hank Smith, and he lived on the other side of town, a half hour away. Once again the prying started, and this time there was an attenuated and earnest squeal, followed finally by a pop just like a balloon, and Martin knew that the front door, off in the darkness of Waterford's practically abandoned main hall, was now standing open, its ancient iron hardware exposed to the air.

His mind was working haphazardly, but the rest of the body went into its precise physiological drill: heart rate up, oxygen intake increased, muscles flexed and ready. Would he stand and fight or run like hell? As Martin hyperventilated, sweat broke out in thousands of pinpricks, and he noticed that he was still holding his drink. Suddenly booze was abhorrent to him. The drinking he had been doing recently seemed to race past his eyes, all those tumblers filled with ice, those tin bottle caps musically unscrewed, that pointless slosh of liquid. Without reflecting he flung aside his glass, and this time there was a shattering sound, as the glass struck the hearth and exploded an amber arc of scotch over the mantel and all over this year's lineup of Christmas cards and snapshots of his newborn grandchild.

He could feel tension in the immediate silence that followed this gesture; bodies, human bodies, unsure. Animals frozen by headlamps; snakes surprised as they basked in the sun. Yes, he felt it, pure life energy flowing in this house now that a confrontation had been announced. It was as if he was getting information through a sixth sense, like a bat with its sonar, or a reptile hearing the sound of heat. For a second or two, he felt that in some fractional way, noise could give him the upper hand. He looked for some other noisemaker: the fireplace shovel. He grabbed for it and clanged a couple of times on the bricks. It made a rather flimsy sound, more like a tin can being crumpled than a sword being drawn, but still, he now had a weapon in his hand. God, he thought, even as he began to advance into the kitchen and toward the swinging door into the main hall, what a caricature! Trying to scare housebreakers away with a highball glass and a fire tool.

Actually, it was more than caricature. He looked down at his clothes, his baby-blue robe and one sock off. Perhaps it was stupid. He glanced at the weapon and stopped walking. He recalled the training that his security consultants gave to new convenience-store managers: Surrender property; don't get between the perpetrator and his escape route. The first time he heard this he almost protested, not that he wanted his employees to get hurt, but wasn't there a way to determine whether the whole thing was a bluff *before* one had given away a storeroom full of his cigarettes and beer? But still, let's get real here: the one way this standoff was certain not to end was with Martin doing battle with a miniature shovel.

He silently cracked open the swinging door enough to peer into the front part of the hall. Everything was still, dark, as untouched as a tomb. Through the dull gloom of this ghostly space he could make out the pompous smirk of Cousin Reginald, posed in his militia regalia. The hall was L-shaped, and Martin could not see around the corner, but the light from behind him cast a gigantic shadow; his exaggerated form covered the wall.

Martin realized that from the front of the house, one could not see the lights in the kitchen and the office; someone had broken in, expecting no one to be home. He hadn't been picking up fallen deadwood on the lawn; who knew what other telltale signs of neglect and abandonment this cat burglar had been able to read from the road? Whoever it was now knew that he'd been wrong. At this point, so the hope goes, the burglar would probably flee. Perhaps he already had, but Martin had to be sure. For the first time it occurred to Martin to use his voice. "Who's there?" he called out sharply.

Perhaps he had not expected to hear anything—he might not have called if he had—but there, at the very end of this pause, yes, a scuff on the carpet, a shifting of weight on the floor, a creak. With a precision that he did not question, he determined that the sound coming to him around the corner originated at the very center of the hall, directly under the crystal chandelier his first wife had installed three decades ago, and which he had been planning to remove and destroy ever since they were divorced. He recognized as well that this person, the housebreaker interrupted in the act, was now looking at six choices of doors to pass through, to hide, or to conceal himself prior to making a jump, to escape, or to attack.

"Just stay where you are," Martin called out again, this time putting an extra bark into it, even trying to sound bored—oh God, another burglar I'll have to throttle. Instead, what he heard in his own voice sounded like a plea; he wanted to sound as if he were forty, savvy and fit, and not like the tired old man he had felt like earlier in the evening. He did not want to sound lonely.

He had been holding the swinging door open a crack in order to shout out these challenges, and when he paused now, the spring gently pushed him back. He could run. He could creep back past his office and to the back door, and then burst out into the windy moonlight, run crazily over obstacles no one else would know to avoid. He could imagine a dozen boyhood hideouts, forts, and spying stations all over the property: the hollow space inside a massive box bush by the lane, a sharp dip in the very center of the vast lawn toward the water where he could vanish from sight. Or he could keep running all the way to the farmyard, where three families, and at least ten dogs, were now sleeping. If it was a false alarm he wouldn't have to feel stupid; he'd often been asked whether it didn't feel spooky living all alone in that big house, whether it was haunted.

Maybe now was the time to admit that, yes, it wasn't good for him to continue his life there, that as it was, all he was doing was waiting to die there. Now that he had run this far, perhaps he could simply slow to a trot and keep going to a new life; call it travel, call it a reward.

Martin had imagined this flight so completely that he was out of breath, but he was still standing on the kitchen side of the swinging door, his nose pressed against the small pane of glass placed there to keep butlers from crashing into each other. He could see no movement in the - half-light, but he knew someone was still there, someone seemingly as frightened as he was. Running wouldn't work.

He opened the door and called out once more, this time with a firm voice. "No one's going to get hurt," he said, taking a few paces, out far enough to reach around to the switch plate. He worked his fingers down the line of buttons to the one that controlled the hall chandelier, and gave it a push.

He remained largely in the darkness, but knew that this overwatted light fixture was in the process of blinding the intruder. He heard a drawing of breath. Yes, a person; he could almost weep with gratefulness, a person, and not a discontented spirit, not a sign of his madness. "I'm reasonable," he said.

"Fuck you, man."

The voice was that of a black man with the thick accent of the Eastern Shore. This was better than it might have been, a local person, and not some pro from Baltimore, and not one of those pasty, bad-toothed, long-haired white men that Amy found so troubling here in the South, big fat arms coming out of workshirts with the sleeves ripped off, their armpits slimy with perspiration. She had feared them as she believed the black population must; she once said to Martin that these are the kind of people that beat up their mothers.

"What are you doing in my house?" Martin said. It wasn't a very clever thing to say, but it got the job done; it kept things going.

"Fuck your house."

Martin could hear a slight rustle and imagined a figure stretching his neck muscles and tendons as he turned to yell in the direction Martin's voice had come to him. Martin was tense and his sweat was flowing, but he realized, to his surprise, that he wasn't as frightened as he had been a few minutes before. Martin took one more step into the hall, and the intruder heard him move.

"You stay the hell where you are." This time, Martin could sense the fear behind these warnings; it was a younger person than he had originally thought, a teenager, a boy, as Martin called any male under twenty. The boy was scared, perhaps not of Martin, but of being caught.

"Fine. Then you can get the hell out."

"You got a gun, man?" The breathing was heavy. "A shotgun or something?"

Martin didn't know what to say. If he said yes, and the
boy had a gun also, they could both be in deep trouble. If
Martin said no, then maybe the boy would just jump him
and beat him up, kill him any old way. Neither scenario
seemed likely, but both seemed possible. As Martin paused
he could hear the sibilant whispers of the boy talking to
himself; perhaps he was having the same debate about the
gun.

"This is stupid," Martin said finally. "No. I don't have a
gun."

"That's good."

"Well, why in hell would I? I don't carry a gun in my
own kitchen." He thought he might add what the security
experts told his employees to say, that he would not fire a
weapon simply to retain property. Martin had not been entirely convinced this point was useful; he wouldn't fight
anyone to save a piece of property, but he might well fight
to keep a piece of property from being stolen. There was a
difference, the fruit of trees that blossomed in the male
side of the Garden. Yet this was precisely the impulse that
the security experts tried to wean out of the clerks in his
stores. Once again there was a long pause, which felt like a
stalemate, and in that mental void Martin found that he
was asking himself whether it was Locke or Hume, or
Hobbes, who thought personal property created the potential for chaos. He tried to remember back to old Geb-
bie's Philo course, at Virginia, and he felt a sudden stab of

longing for this knowledge now lost. Martin had sparkled as a student in Charlottesville; his room on the Lawn in Jefferson's campus had been a hangout for serious—if pretentious—student poets and certain junior faculty members. Such a long time ago.

"I don't know nothing about you, man."

"Then what are you doing here?" Martin was still too frightened to sit down, but his legs felt rubbery and he eyed the side chair beside the table, directly under the light switches. With a small jolt, he realized he had almost never sat in this chair, but his mother often had, taking her place at the geographic center of the house while cleaning ladies cleaned and cooks cooked, and Martin played. He was twelve when she died, and it was not a mystery to him, or to his two wives, or to his three children, or, indeed, to a therapist in Easton once briefly consulted, that losing his mother at that age had been the great tragedy of his life, and that short of losing one of his children, nothing would ever equal it. His mother had a soft Charleston lilt in her voice, and a beauty and a style that were still remembered fondly by people all over the South. Monique Jamaica Grey was how she signed everything, using the middle name given to her by a rather roguish father in the place of her maiden name after she was married. As an infant, Martin had first become aware of her as a fragrance, a combination of soap and perfume—some secret recipe that she wore all her life—and now he could smell it all over again, whether real or imagined it did not matter, the sense went straight through his memory to his heart.

"What are you, anyway, some kind of hermit? Lights ain't on; place looks like a wreck."

The voice had lost much of its menace, but on top of this emerging deep memory of his mother, the words struck Martin as undeserved insults. He couldn't bear the thought of either of his parents seeing him these past few months; he was an only child, and their love and approval meant everything, even now. He snarled back an answer. "Just because the grass is long you think that's an invitation to come strip the place?"

"You going to let me go or not?"

"I told you. I don't have a gun."

"Well what then? You going to call the sheriff? You gonna try to get my tag number? Try some downtown shit?"

These were good questions, although Martin wasn't entirely sure what "downtown" might mean to a kid raised on the Eastern Shore. "How old are you?" he asked.

This question seemed to surprise him, or, at least, to make him think. In fact, the boy did not answer it. Instead, he said, "What difference that make?"

In other words, concluded Martin, he was about the age Martin thought: sixteen, seventeen. Martin was not unrealistic enough to let it calm him, but this *was* only a boy. He had probably bought candy at one of Martin's stores, ice cream and soda, one of those mute and skittish figures, white and black, who brought their money from deep in their jeans, and some of whom—you could never predict which by the way they dressed—would finally meet your eye and say Thank you when the deal was done, sometimes even Thank you, sir, or ma'am. And yes, some of those kids turned out bad, and hurt people, usually themselves most of all. Wasn't that the way of it? Martin would almost have liked to lecture this boy, tell him that one was perhaps doled out a certain amount of life, a finite number of heartbeats, like beads at a Club Med, to spend however one wants. Tell him that there is someday a turn in life that can give us a glimpse of what will be written on our tombstones.

But what of himself? Two thirds of his life was over, but a third remained. In anything else but life, that wouldn't seem so bad, it would seem like plenty. So why was he sitting here in this big family tomb, drinking night after night? Who was he to advise this child about anything?

"You still there?"

"Yes," said Martin.

"How old are *you*?"

The question was meant to taunt him, to be fresh and aggressive and sarcastic, but at the last second, on the "you," the boy had added an upturn that might almost be considered sweet. Because of this, Martin found himself saying, "I'm fifty-nine. I've got three kids that are probably older than you." Martin didn't know why, but he went on to tell this boy that he owned a convenience store—he admitted to just one—and that he expected he'd sold candy to him in the past. Martin guessed he was doing this in order to scare the boy, make him wonder if his voice could be identified by Martin in a lineup, though he wasn't sure. Who could not have some sympathy for a child who broke into houses at one in the morning, even if it's your own house? Martin had been raised to think like that, to give his trust freely, like offering rides to dusty people walking along the shoulder of the highway. His father was a trusting man, which had been for the most part easy for him to do. He came from a life that owned virtually everything in sight, and what he didn't own, but wanted, he could trust that he would acquire. It was trust, of course, that had led him to marry his second wife, Evelyn, to take "a turn for the nurse," as his old law firm partner, Beveridge Bartlett, had said. God knew that Evelyn had made his last years more comfortable and, certainly, easier on Martin; God knew as well that Evelyn could have run off with a great deal of the estate, and not simply accepted the final settlement and left quietly and unexpectedly one day in June, twenty years ago. Martin didn't know whether she was still alive, but he suspected that she might be, in her early eighties, in Florida.

"What store?"

"What?"

"What convenience store? The Only Stop? The one on Route Fifty?"

"Yes, as a matter of fact. The Only Stop on Route Fifty." Martin tried to recall whether this store had been held up recently, and he didn't think it had. In fact, burglaries didn't happen all that much in any of them, just a lot of shoplifting and pilferage, and a fair amount of "shrinkage," as he had learned to call it, which referred to the quantities of stuff hauled home by his trusted and valued employees. What they took seemed so unnecessary to life—charcoal briquettes, of all things, seemed to "shrink" more than anything.

"A shithole," said the boy.

"Now wait a goddamn minute. What are you calling a shithole. My store?" This did hurt. Go into any grimy WaWa or 7-Eleven, he wanted to say, and tell me my Only Stop is a shithole. Still, to this day, Martin himself had trouble with the knowledge that, along with the lottery tickets, his stores tended to fulfill the worst needs of his customers. He had wondered once whether, in terms of cancer caused by his cigarettes and traffic accidents caused by his beer, one might be able to calculate the precise cost to society of his business. He sold a lot of condoms, which was fine by him, and newspapers, but the other convenience items, the milk, eggs, Kraft macaroni and cheese, and breakfast cereals, they were overpriced; he'd see teenage mothers and ancient black gentlemen doing grocery shopping and he'd have to force himself not to encourage them to shop more wisely. Martin owned a store right down on the tip of Cape Charles in Virginia, on Route 13, and it was the only place for the tiny local population to buy such groceries for many miles, and Martin had been thinking for years that he should offer a once-a-week shuttle-bus service up to Salisbury for these people, so they could avoid his own monopoly.

Martin realized that Only Stop was not the issue of the hour. Now it was his turn to bring them back to reality. "What's the plan here? You leave, right? I keep my eyes closed for a count of one hundred?" The boy gave a slight grunt. "Then who's going to fix my door?"

"Fuck your door. Fix it yourself. You got the money."

Martin liked the squabbling; it felt like discourse. It made him begin to trust that none of this would have to turn out badly for anyone.

"Listen, I'm willing to let the door go," he said, speaking now as he used to when his own kids were little, and when they had broken things, like the time they wiped out a line of crystal goblets with a football. He didn't yell at them; he asked why were they playing football in the dining room. He had no reason to push it farther, and no reason now either. Why become a force against this child, facing a world in which there were so many barriers anyway. Here, finally, the security experts could make some sense: Don't make trouble for others if they don't make trouble for you. The next morning Lavell McClelland would come over and repair the door in a way that was historically pure and staggeringly expensive. Martin tried to think of the next thing to say, but nothing came to him, nothing but the need that had been growing these past few minutes, the need to be liked by someone—by this boy especially. As soon as he admitted this to himself, he knew that any second the boy would bolt, and that would be the end to it.

"What's the deal with all this old stuff?" the voice suddenly asked.

"What stuff?"

"All this old shit. What's the deal with it?"

"No deal. It's family stuff."

Martin could hear scuffing on the floor; the boy was turning around in his spot. "Who's this broad with the feathers on her head?"

He was talking about Abigail Heintz Grey, 1722–1764. Her husband, Charles, had built the wing of Waterford in which they were standing. Who knew whether Abigail had lived a happy life here? Probably not. Still, the portraitist had dressed her up in a rather vampy costume, a drawstring of blue satin partially gathering the top of her bodice, a milky chest and a neck as long as a pedestal; the rest of the costume was ostrich feathers, or a boa, or something like that. Martin had always liked this painting and once, as a teenager, had been successful in masturbating to it, although, he recalled, it took a lot of imagination. "She's someone who used to live here, a couple of hundred years ago."

The boy wouldn't know what to do with this portrait if he stole it, any more than Martin knew what to do with it if he didn't. Just leave it hanging there for another hundred years, and for what? Martin thought of his friends—if that's what he could call them—up and down the Shore, peering out their windows at night with the vague fear that their houses were being watched. They'd recall the dry cleaner delivery boy of the other day, the one they'd never seen before, or the two Hispanics that appeared last fall looking for work. At cocktail parties—oh God, never, ever again—they'd be talking about drug runners, so they had heard, plying the coves and creeks in speedboats without running lights. They'd remember the celebrated cases of crimes in farm country, the ones they read about in the fifties, Charlie Starkweather, the men from *In Cold Blood*. God, thought Martin, the rich on the Eastern Shore, in those big houses on the Corsica, the Chester, the Miles, and the Tred Avon, they'd be fools if they didn't worry now and again. There are people out there who don't wish them well.

So there it was: his life, his people, his future. Martin let out the biggest sigh of his life. It started a foot below his heart, started at the far side of his organs and drew upwards, gathering the emotional detritus and spiritual de-

bris of all of the disappointments and losses that had been
on his mind this evening, as well as all those other fears and
anxieties that had not been on his mind, arranged these living, internal demons into an orderly line in his windpipe,
and then ushered them out into the air. It must have made
quite a sound, this cry from the gut. No one hearing it
would guess how good it felt.

"You know, man, you're a *mess*. You sitting here in this
big house, drinking all alone. I can smell the liquor on
your breath from here."

Well, thought Martin, that settles it. Right here. Right
now. Call it epiphany. Call it hitting bottom. Call it one
last chance, or call it just the next step. Time to take it.
Bells. Whistles. A slap in the face, and did he ever need
that. He started to laugh, and it felt so good, though
slightly hysterical, that he kept going with it. "A mess," he
roared a couple of times. "Phew," he said when he was
done.

There was a long silence, and then, "I'm getting out of
here. You still going to let me go?"

"I'll make a deal with you."

"What deal it?"

"I'll turn the light off. You can go. But don't shoplift
anything from my store. Don't make stupid choices, like
breaking into a house in the middle of the night." He
flicked the lights off, and moved a step forward to sit down
in the chair. A deep and dense darkness descended upon

him. His chest cavity was sore with laughter, cleansed, and in that moment of peace, he thought of Amy. It was perhaps not too late, in the night or in their marriage, for him to call her now, to tell her what had happened. He started to recite her telephone number: 2-1-2-8-3—

Suddenly he was aware of movement. A scuffling, darting figure just barely in his peripheral vision, and then there was a hand raised with something in it, and that hand dropped, collided with his skull, and sent him open-mouthed and dazed onto the floor.

He felt the pain from his carpet-burned cheek before he was aware of any other sensation. He was face down, splayed flat. He was terrified that he would soon feel the sticky warm flow of his own blood, seeping into the wool beneath him. With fear and with difficulty, he drew one of his hands to the source of his pain, behind his neck, and all he felt was a dry lump. In relief, he dropped his hand back to his side, and when he did, he saw the dark shadow above him.

This could very well be the end, he thought. The boy could kill him now, with Martin never knowing exactly why. He asked, "What did you do that for?"

"For laughing at me, you white bastard."

"It wasn't you. Please go," he added, but he was talking to no one. The boy was already gone, just a visitation now, perhaps not even real, a messenger from the dark.

A Suitable Good-bye

Lee Nichols, his mother, Ruth, and his eleven-year-old nephew, Ranger, stood their ground in the waiting hall of Pennsylvania Station. Their train was due to be announced at any moment, and Ruth had first suggested, then insisted, Lee take the bags in hand. She and the boy had flown in from Pittsburgh that morning, and the ritual mode of transportation she had selected for this part of the trip struck Lee as both novel and archaic, like the clattering departure board above his head that sent out its information in frantic shufflings of plastic cards. Lee glanced around him, at the knots of people with eyes trained on the board. His presumed fellow passengers for this iron dash into the Deep South, to Mississippi, of all places, were mostly people with children or elderly parents, or both, whole families on the move, perhaps to weddings or funerals. The Nicholses were not marrying or burying anyone, but this was a family mission.

Lee was thirty-seven, a freelance consultant on corporate communications: copywriting, writing seminars, a video here or there. Over the years his mother had occasionally revealed her fears when she described him as being "unemployed"; the word, he explained to her, was "self-employed." These days he was not "in a good way," as he had admitted to his girlfriend, Tina, recently. His life, as it had all too often done in the past, was hinging on an overdue check, and if he did not get a go-ahead on his latest project proposal—he expected an answer any day, any hour—he could hardly imagine how he would survive the month. He was going crazy, hounding the mailbox and his answering machine. So when his mother called just two days earlier and said she had in mind a "mad mission" and wondered if he could take some time to accompany her, he pretended to consult his calendar, and then agreed.

"I had not expected such a crowd," she said. She wrinkled her nose at the oppressive smell, rancid oil and popcorn, body heat, ammonia. Her hand darted from opposite wrist, to blazer lapel, to neckline and ears, checking for each piece of her family's golden past.

Lee smiled: for her, only an assemblage of the lower classes constituted a "crowd." Many of her words were part of a code, which she believed allowed her to speak her prejudices without getting caught. He had come to find this endearing. He put his arm jocularly around her shoulders. "This isn't the Twentieth Century Limited," he said. "People ride the train because it's cheap."

She removed his heavy forearm and turned to Ranger. "Pay attention. Don't let your backpack get out there in the crowd."

Ranger was a milky boy with fuzzy brown hair, so soft around the waist that his belt cut a deep furrow in his flesh. He seemed incapable of standing squarely in front of an adult. Lee had not known that his nephew had been invited along until Ranger appeared at Ruth's side at the airport. Ruth had been moving him around like a shopping cart all day, which the boy didn't appear to mind: walking in one direction on his own or being pushed in another by her hand on his backpack seemed all the same to him. Lee found himself wondering what the boy's parents, his brother, Rick, and Alicia, really felt about having such an awkward kid, and what they had done to create one. Lee tried to act like an uncle—friendly, ironical, lax on manners—but it was difficult for him, a man who knew nothing about children.

"Relax," he said, turning back to his mother. "Our roomettes are reserved."

"I'll relax when everything is settled—"

"Perfect," he said, cutting her off. "The theme for the trip."

"Stop it." She glared at this, but she loved to be teased. "I suppose going all this way to locate my father's grave is

macabre for you." At the time of her father's death, a sui-
cide in 1942, the family had been living in Hattiesburg,
Mississippi. She added, darkly and not without self-pity,
"But at my age . . ."

His mother still looked stunning: her face had great
bones and her skin was white and smooth; his girlfriends
always commented on his mother's looks. He noticed the
even line of her tweed skirt hem, her sheer stockings and
simple blue heels. He thought of her dressing like this,
every day, the time it took, the careful layering of cotton,
nylon, silk, and wool, ending with makeup and jewelry,
and with a last combing of her sculpted hair. It seemed
blissfully old-fashioned, making such preparations for days
that could be so uneventful. Her father, a joyless and distracted man, a professor of English, had apparently put on
a dinner jacket every night of his adult life, even when he
dined alone.

Lee turned the other way, and caught Ranger staring at
him. The boy's pale eyes flickered, seemed ready again to
duck and dart, but they did not, they stayed on Lee and
seemed, finally, to be asking for encouragement. Lee
hardly knew where to begin. He wondered how the boy
handled his school, a country day, how he did with the
other boys. Perhaps not all that well. From deep in his
heart, Lee tried to return a warm smile, a cheering reference to all those wider goods and rewards that he himself
had such difficulty keeping in mind. As soon as the con-
jured expression—who knew what it actually looked

like?—reached Lee's face, the boy's eyes took sudden fright and diverted, and then the departure board above them began furiously searching its storehouse of letters and numbers.

Lee had just finished getting settled into his roomette—Ruth and the boy were sharing a family bedroom—when his mother banged on the beige partition and came through the heavy olive-drab day curtain. She was holding a spiral steno pad, one of her "notebooks": Lee's entire life, and those of his father and siblings, had been charted, catalogued, and accounted for in a succession of many hundreds of these books.

"So," he said, "let's hear the agenda." He gave this a gently mocking spin, as she brought the pad up to her chest and riffled through the pages.

"Mon. night on train," she read quickly, sharing her own form of shorthand. "Arrive Tue. four PM in H-burg." She stopped, and lowered the book in order to fix him in her sight. "I'm giving us two days to find the grave. Do you think that is enough?"

Ruth had been away for her first year at Pitt when her father died, and she had not been able, in the wartime economy, to arrange transportation back in time for the funeral. Her mother and aunt, it seemed to Lee, had packed up and left town within a week or two, making an end to several bad pieces of luck. Neither the man nor the place had been much mourned. The family had lived in Hattiesburg for nearly twenty years while her father taught at the university, and the whole time Ruth's mother and aunt had stalwartly remained transplanted natives of Pittsburgh. It had even been a family joke to compare the great city associated forever with the noble William Pitt to a modest rail hub and lumber town solipsistically named by a surveyor after his wife, Hattie. The proof of the older women's efforts was that the child, Ruth, grew up without one hint of a Southern accent. This was the first time anyone, as far as Lee knew, had made this trip back.

"Lee?" she said, interrupting his distracted silence. "I've tried to organize this carefully so you won't have to rush back."

"I know. Don't worry."

"This way you won't be away too long. That was the trouble with Martha's wedding. It went on too long."

"Oh, please," he said. Two years earlier, in the midst of family, aunts and uncles and children by the tens, he had ducked out right after the ceremony of his sister's wedding. Though later he had apologized all around, he still did not understand why his absence had caused so much hurt and anger; he had honestly believed that the rest of the family could have more fun without having to make a place for the odd man out, the single one, the cynical one. "Let's not go into that," he said now. She nodded, closed her notebook, and, the business done, the plan set, backed out through the partition.

He pulled out the complimentary Amtrak stationery packet, complete with an old-fashioned retractable ball-point pen, whose unusual plastic smell, sharp and sweet, reminded him of a set of twenty colored pens that he had redeemed for two box tops and two quarters long ago. He had no quarrel with his childhood, not with his father, who had given all his labor and heart to his duties as he had received and understood them, and certainly not with his mother. Many people found her imperious, but Lee's best friends, and those of his brother and sisters, realized soon enough that most of her orders and barks were meant ironically. If, in the end, Lee had drifted far away, the fault might lie in something as simple and inescapable as his birth order in the family, somewhere in the middle of the pack, a sibling without portfolio.

He looked out his window as the train slowed for its brief stop in Newark and then soon, far sooner than he would have imagined, they were rolling through a pleasant landscape of farms and suburban housing. He was refreshed by this view, by the shine of a brilliant midafternoon in February, clear as the Arctic. Even along the grimy tracksides there were pines and hemlocks flocked with a light morning snow. How much he had forgotten about the countryside during his many years in Manhattan.

And how much else had passed him by? He seemed, lately, to be asking himself just this kind of question, questions of quantity, as if there were a calculus that could help him understand his life. He had begun to recognize that the way he lived—by his wits, as his sister Ginnie had so chillingly summed it up—was expensive, that the overhead of anxiety and pressure had to be paid for somehow. Each time he sank into depression he emerged feeling that it had cost him too much to recover.

At dinner, they were shown to a table with a stained salmon-colored tablecloth and a purple bud vase. There was no flower in the vase, which made Lee assume that it had been real and was now being worn on a lapel, or behind an ear, in the lounge car.

"Sit there," Ruth said to Ranger. All Lee had seen or heard of him, as they were drinking their cocktails in the smoky lounge, was the bristly top of his head and the staccato popping of his video game's beeps and reports.

"Blame Grammy on your father and me," said Lee. "We never stuck up for our rights and she got used to bossing us around."

The boy gave him a slight smile and then glanced fearfully at Ruth.

"Don't pay attention to Uncle Lee," she said. They read their menus for a moment or two, and then Ruth told the boy to order the lamb chops.

"Let him have what he wants," said Lee.

"Well, certainly," she answered, flustered. "Of course he can have what he wants."

Lee watched, unsurprised, as the boy shrugged helplessly and let the order for the lamb chops stand. The waiter, uninterested in this family unit, stood with his pencil raised while Lee considered the menu one last time and then, eyes on his mother, ordered the spaghetti and meatballs.

"Oh, Lee. You know it will be dreadful!"

"Of course it will." He smiled, and because Ranger had looked up quickly, he winked at the boy. "I like dreadful food," he added, and his mind jumped back to his kitchen in New York. His sister Ginnie, the only member of his family who knew how he really lived, had observed long ago that his apartment was the most unloved home she'd ever seen. She was right about the inattention, but the truth was that Lee had never thought of the place as "home" anyway.

It was dark outside, a winter dusk settling on a smooth Virginia landscape; they were slowing for Manassas, and later the trainman announced Culpepper in a deep, black-timbred voice. Lee remarked that this was quite pleasant, dining as they rolled through all this history. Then the waiter appeared with their dinners and dropped them, literally, into place. Lee exchanged his spaghetti for Ranger's lamb chops. From the surprised and grateful look he got in return, he realized that boyhood had not changed all that much in thirty years.

Happy with his supper, unmindful of the small red splatters that were accumulating on his white shirt and on the tablecloth around his plate, Ranger made a pleasant companion through dinner. Lee was cheered by spending time with a child and with his mother, age groups so foreign to his normal life, the narrow band of hucksters and achievers that he knew in New York. Ranger became fidgety after he finished his sundae, and Ruth released him to their room. She called him back twice, first to retrieve his video game, and then, when he had almost reached the end of the car, to tell him to brush his teeth.

"He just needs . . . a little more spine," she said. "Don't you think?"

"How would I know?" answered Lee.

"Perhaps you wouldn't," she agreed. "But I always thought you would make a good father."

Lee heard this with disbelief. He knew she sincerely wanted to think such a generous thought about him, but he wondered how much of anything she said to him, or to any other of her progeny, she actually believed.

"I do wish Frank would help more," she admitted, referring to Lee's sister Martha's husband. Both of Lee's sisters were adjusting to newborns, and Lee had been hearing more than he wanted to hear about juggling career and motherhood.

"Please," he said. "Skip the babies." As he spoke he recalled that being told to "skip it" had always infuriated her.

"I said nothing about the children," she answered sharply. "I was talking about your sisters." She reached across the table to fold up the linen napkin that Ranger had tied into a tight, whip-like spiral. "Don't be disagreeable.

Everyone asks about your news, you know. Ginnie was so disappointed that job—what was it?—didn't come through for you."

Lee let this line of conversation drop, and noticed that she was fiddling ever so slightly and nervously with the packets of sugar. She had raised them to understand that such nervous tics revealed deep character flaws.

"Mom," he said. "What's the program for this trip? Why are we here? Why Ranger?"

She produced a surprised and hurt look. "I need your help. I don't feel quite so confident heading off as I once did." She reached for her purse and withdrew her compact, which she opened and held before her in her left hand, powder pad in her right, as if waiting for him to break her heart and ruin her makeup.

"Ranger and me," said Lee. "We're just your two lost sheep. We're the ones on the worry list. Right?"

"Don't be silly. In fact, I thought it would be good for Ranger to spend some time with you. Rick and Alicia take everything so seriously. They aren't teaching him irony."

"But that doesn't mean this isn't a salvage trip."

"Can't I worry about you? Is there some law against it? You haven't introduced me to your new girlfriend. You never give the rest of us your news. And that work of yours—"

"It's a profession," he interrupted. "It's . . ." What? he wondered for a few seconds. "It's what I do."

He left it at that, trying to suggest that his work was the

only concern she had raised. He knew how much she wanted to hear good things about the rest of his life: that he might marry Tina, or was considering moving out of the city to someplace nice, or that he had accepted an offer to teach English at a prep school. Even something smaller, the smallest shred of change, could have served as a suitable apology for the years of worry he had caused her. But there was no candied hope to give her, even if he might have wished there were.

"I'm just trying to offer you some support," she said. "Even Rick's business is slow these days," she added.

"Even Rick! Well, I'll be."

She had exhausted her repertoire of wordless retorts, and Lee, feeling rather tired himself, had not put any real feeling into his last statement. For years she had shielded him from Rick's accomplishments; the family news used to come to him like a newspaper doctored for a sequestered jury, with long strips of air in the place of the latest headline on IBM's boy wonder. But Lee had never believed that he and his brother were competing in the same sport. His mother reached for the check and he sat feeling diminished as she paid. They lurched forward through three cars, each time greeted with the roar of the air scented with diesel exhaust, and he bid her good night in the corridor, holding on to the handrails for a kiss on the cheek as the train rattled and slammed its way south.

Lee closed the sliding door behind him, lowered the bed, stripped and slid into the cool sheets, read for an hour and then reached up to turn off the final pleasant glow of the thoughtfully placed reading lamp. He forced himself not to worry whether the check had come in the late mail; it was enough to know that working hours were over, that bookkeepers had long ago gone home, and that transactions processed before they left would not mean anything until tomorrow. He felt secure, with his life in the leather-gloved hands of the engineer eight cars ahead, the father of the train with eyes fixed on a future illuminated by the locomotive's twin lamps. If the check had not arrived, perhaps it was now, at this very moment, being handled and conveyed toward the right bag for delivery tomorrow, salvation working its way toward his doorstep in a No. 10 envelope. It was as if he could make it so by visualizing the delivery in minute detail, his own form of prayer.

He was wide awake. He sat up and turned on the light. He began a letter to Tina, his girlfriend, and he told her that the trip had so far gone as he would have supposed, except for the inclusion of his nephew. "The two endangered ones of my mother's brood," he wrote. "She may have a point."

A freight, inches from his window, met his train with the thud of colliding tidal waves of air; he jumped and watched for a moment as the silver countryside showed itself in narrow instant slivers between the box cars and then the black freight was gone with a vacant hiss. They were passing through hilly terrain, the steep-sided valleys of the lower Shenandoah, and under the cold moon, the breasts of the winter meadows seemed new and untouched. He reached for his Amtrak ballpoint again. "From what I have told you," he wrote to his lover, "you might not realize how kind my family has been to me. They have all found more ways to let me off the hook than the world's worst fly caster. This time I don't want to let my mother down. That's the mission for the week."

He slept terribly. Each time the train slowed and braked for a station his head met the partition and vibrations passed through his skull. When he awoke, sore and damp in the processed air, it was almost nine o'clock. He washed and bathed the best he could in the tiny vessel of his fold-down lavatory, and backed out of his cabin to find Ranger lurking in the corridor. The boy had been standing in this sunless and cold metal hallway for who knew how long, as patient as a sled dog.

"Good morning . . . Ranger," he said, using this name for the first time. He knew that Ruth would have eaten breakfast much earlier, and would now be writing letters. All it takes to keep in touch, she had once airily advised, is a couple of hours a day.

Ranger looked at his feet.

"What's up?" Lee started to say, but then it occurred to him that the boy had been waiting for him. "Come on," he waved and three cars later, they were seated on the left side of the train in a flood of yellow sun.

"Uncle Lee? Please don't call me Ranger. I hate it."

Lee lowered his menu and looked over at the boy.

"Kids tease me about it. Can you call me Richard? Please?"

This time, making this declaration, the eyes were steady and the face free of apology. Lee could not think of anything to say without sounding patronizing. "You don't have to call me Uncle Lee," he answered finally. "We've got that straight. Lee and Richard."

Lee kept the conversation going—So how is school, anyway?—and found it actually not all that difficult. The food came, and Richard dug into his stack of pancakes, another timeless choice, timeless for Lee. It occurred to him that he had not had breakfast, alone, with an eleven-year-old since he himself was that age. He found pleasure in nourishing this child, and understood for the first time those looks of supreme contentment on the faces of mothers when their children were eating a good supper. Lee did not dislike children, as his sister Martha had once claimed: he just didn't know enough about them to feel comfortable with them, which was perhaps a personal failing or perhaps something more darkly male.

The boy felt Lee staring at him and looked up from his breakfast. Lee felt caught, and said the first thing that came to mind. "Look, Richard. You and me, we're Grammy's project for the week."

"Yeh, I heard my mom talking about it."

"So while she's solving all our problems, let's have some fun."

After breakfast Richard came back to Lee's roomette, and was happy enough to sit on the padded footrest and stare out the window. Lee was surprised, as he read, to hear a strange faint sound, and then realized that Richard was singing to himself, humming some little tune over the drone of the train noise, and Lee was touched to share this self-contained amusement. The train had left behind the openness of Georgia's red fields, and for a time the landscape alternated between rolling farmland and a living tunnel of winter plant life, of moss, fern, and magnolia. Through the heart of the day they worked across Alabama and Mississippi. It seemed to Lee many days ago that they had departed the oily concrete terrain of the northern cities. As time passed Richard interrupted with a few "look at that"s, and then nearly fell on the floor with laughter when he saw a man chasing three pigs down the main street of a dusty little farm town. The laugh was rich and unchecked. Lee looked up quickly enough to see a bit of the scene himself. He gave up on his book and, side by side with the boy, devoted his attention to the passing panorama of decaying spur-line mills, ornamented with clock towers and fancy brick corbeling, and to the intimacy of family scenes they grabbed as the train sped past back yards and grade crossings. They pulled into Hattiesburg as the sun began to take on the reddish invitations of evening, and Lee realized that for the first time in months, or maybe even years, he had gone through a full day without once worrying about money.

They had arrived, it seemed, in the deserted back end of a crumbling community. A soft breeze, the pillowed coolness of southern winter, hit him with a smooth slap. The air was soupy with the fermented odors of lumber and sawdust. The platform was a long stretch of concrete, broken up with meandering lines of browned grasses.

"Well," Ruth said bravely, adjusting her large straw hat against the flat rays of last light, "we all certainly have aged."

"It's really quite charming," he said, looking ahead at the unusual sight, to Northern eyes, of a white man and a black man, two taxi drivers, chatting amiably over the hood of a battered Checker. "This is most definitely not Manhattan."

She did not answer, and Lee began to worry that the long train ride was causing her some kind of collapse. Even though he suspected all things would be done differently down here, he hailed the drivers with the short piercing whistle he had perfected in flush times when he took cabs in New York, and the white one came out to give him a hand. "Welcome to Hattiesburg," he said. "The hub city of Mississippi."

They drove through a pleasant historic center and then

passed a grand columned brick building, a Georgian temple, that appeared to mark the heart of the university. This was the kind of city, Lee thought, that places high on national rankings for livability, with special mention for health care and convenient shopping. His mother looked intently out the window and made a show of pointing out the sights, but she kept on being corrected by the taxi driver, who could not see her glaring at him from the back seat. She stood back while Lee checked them in to their hotel, and quite without thinking, he put the boy with him and gave the single to his mother. It seemed only reasonable. The look the boy gave him, as they entered their room, was close to triumphant.

Lee opened the nubby drape to reveal the parking lot of a Piggly Wiggly, a strip of fast-food joints, and the heedless slash of an interstate. While Richard pawed through the individual-sized complimentary toiletries and then brewed Lee a cup of instant coffee, Lee took up the phone and dialed his office. The first message on his machine was from a graphic designer about a job that was winding down, for which he had long ago been paid, and she used the word "fuck" twice in her message, without irony or apology. New York, he thought: what a pretty place it is. The second message was from his job prospect. "Call me tomorrow," the man said. "I'll only be in for a few minutes at twelve." Lee hung up and went through the process to hear the messages twice more, first the profanities, and then the "call me," a positive tone to it, the sound of a man who just might be able to say yes.

They ate dinner in an Elizabethan-inspired steak house a few doors down from the Ramada, passing the time on Ruth's memories of a proper Victorian house, bounded by a meticulously maintained wooden fence with swooping lines of pickets between posts topped with urns. "It's odd," she said, "but I remember that fence far more vividly than the house. Symbolic, I suppose," she added, and Lee could only agree. The pleasures she recalled in this cheerless and circumscribed home were of the tiniest scope: using a squashed raspberry to rouge her doll, and then being punished by her aunt. She recalled being served iced tea on the porch as the family waited for her father to return from the university. Lee had once asked her, hearing such stories, if she had a single recollection of being alone, anywhere or anytime, before the age of fifteen, and she thought hard before admitting that she did not. Even into her late teens, her mother used to give her books to read with notes sprinkled through saying "Stop reading here and skip to page 422," orders that she followed without protest.

"You really don't like being here, do you?" asked Lee. They were walking back to the motel, and she had taken his arm. It was clear to him that she had become steadily less cheerful and more fragile from the moment they left Penn Station.

"I don't think anyone likes this kind of return," she said, as if he would be surprised to learn that she thought so. It wasn't her way to admit to unhappiness.

"Then why are we here? You never liked your father. No one did, as far as I can tell."

"That doesn't have anything to do with it. He's been alone all these years."

"I don't think he's noticed, Mom. Even when he was alive he didn't sound all that aware."

She breathed a resigned but forgiving sigh. "I know, dear. This is all ancient history to you. It's prehistoric to the children," she said, beckoning toward Richard and finishing with a shrug. "Your father thinks it's mad too, but I've really got no choice. It just isn't an option for me to finish my life without saying good-bye to my father."

"Farewell, Dad? Sorry you took the longest drive of your life?"

"Now Lee."

"Or good riddance? I hope you went to hell?"

She gave his arm a squeeze to silence him, but she did not deny that there could be much bitterness in this trip.

"I'm just trying to understand exactly what you are hoping to accomplish here."

"I've never understood why your generation, for all the free thinking it espouses, seems to think everything needs a reason. It's 'closure'; isn't that what you all call it? I want to do this and get it over with, and I'm happy you're with me."

"So am I, Mom. I'm glad you asked me."

When they got back to their hotel room, Richard found a chocolate mint on his pillow. "This is great," he said, peeling off the foil. "We're just in time for *Terminator 2*."

Lee took off his shoes and called down for room service. He had been looking forward to seeing this movie all during dinner. He was surprised, for a moment, that Richard chose to stretch out beside him on the same bed, close enough for Lee to feel the heat of this small body. He could feel the need and the trust, the youngest member of the tribe attaching himself to the one he believed would protect him.

When room service answered he ordered beer and Coke, potato chips and Cheez Doodles. "Having a kid around is a great excuse to eat junk and watch trash movies," he said.

Richard looked confused. "I thought you had kids."

Lee began to make a joke of this, but he stopped: he felt a sudden, almost sharp, stab of hurt. How little this boy knew of him; how little his brother and sister-in-law must have said about him over the years. Mysterious Uncle Lee, the one who always arrived last and left first. He answered that he had been married once, to a woman named Alice, but they had not had children.

"Gee," said the boy. Being a kid, he couldn't imagine a life without them. They were watching previews now. Richard let his reasoning wander. "Mom says you avoid us but I think that's okay."

"She does?"

"Yeah. She says you're always looking for the door. How come?"

Lee's answer came right out. "I'm just one of those people that always feel trapped. You know what I mean? Sometimes it's kind of a problem for me being around people."

"Yeh. Mom says if I just paid a little more attention to kids my age I'd have more friends."

"Listen to your mom. It's good advice," said Lee, taking the boy's hand.

In the morning, they left the Ramada with a list of the churchyards that were most likely to have received the remains of this suicide, so many years ago. Ruth had developed this list over several weeks of discussions with the Registry of Graves and with funeral homes. It could be any one of them; their family had not been religious in the least. She had tried calling some of the churches but had quickly become exasperated with the volunteers and other kindly souls who answered the phones and then lost her in transit. A mere week ago she had given up, and had decided the best way to find and visit the grave was to do it all at once, in person.

Their plan, as much as they had discussed it, was to locate her old home and move outward. As promised by the Ramada brochure, the university and the faculty neighborhoods were only a few minutes distant, and once they had broken away from the commerce of Hardy Street they were rewarded with the cool gray shadows of bare walnuts and oaks and the rattle of a slight breeze through magnolia leaves. It was going to be a very mild day, but the sunlight was still white and wintry; the combination was disorienting to Lee and made him think of global warming. A number of the houses on these streets needed paint, and in one or two cases most of the ornaments and turnings had been stripped off and replaced by naked boards. But when at last they approached the right street, they were confronted with the most meticulously maintained building in the neighborhood, with a white fence bordering the property like embroidery, and at the same time that Ruth was exclaiming that this, finally, was her childhood home, Lee was concluding that only a funeral parlor would look this good. And then a large, though tasteful, sign, HUMPHREY-HAWKINS FUNERAL ASSOCIATES, became readable in the front yard ahead of them.

Lee and his mother both gasped, and she held her breath for so long that Lee worried she might pass out. "Now this is just killing," she said, finally exhaling.

A hearse started to pull slowly away from the porte cochere. "Well, you have to say it's strangely appropriate."

"An *undertaker* lives here?" asked Richard.

Lee put his hand around the boy's neck and muzzled him. "How does it look?" he asked his mother.

"Quite the same," she answered glumly. "I wish we

could just get this over with and then have some fun together."

They were not dismayed when they struck out at the
first church, with a sexton who had all the records on a
personal computer. The second church was Baptist—very
unlikely—and it turned out to be not much more than a
chapel with only about thirty graves. A discordant ladies'
choir, with a spindly soprano soloist, was working painfully
through an anthem as they strolled past the headstones.
They came back out on Hardy Street and decided to drop
into a Dunkin' Donuts to regroup.

"I really think it must be the Episcopal one," she said.
Richard was attempting to stuff an entire honey-dip donut
into his mouth at once. She reached over and pulled his
hand backward until his teeth were poised for a more polite mouthful. "It seems quite big," she said, referring to
the church.

Lee nodded; she looked tired, too tired to be wandering
through graveyards. This whole thing was starting to
anger him, her compulsion to pay this final obeisance to
the man who had taken a long, leisurely drive in his Stude-
baker without opening the garage door, and without so
much as a note to his daughter. The man didn't deserve
her love, or her steadfastness, whatever it was. Lee wanted
to say this, even to enumerate all the ways it seemed he had
neglected her even when he was alive, but it was suddenly
clear to Lee that he could not do this. He could not pretend to righteousness. He could almost see the dead man

pointing a skeletal finger back at him and asking *And what of you, young man? Do you deserve her love?*

At the Episcopal church they were again unsuccessful. The building was well maintained, gray limestone accented with courses of deep red; the parish house, as Lee had now learned to call it, had been recently renovated. Though no enterprising committee had placed the records "on line," all burial information had been cross-referenced by date and last name, and neither gave evidence of Professor Schaeffer.

"This wasn't supposed to be easy," Lee reminded Ruth as they walked back out.

"No. It wasn't," she said. She was pushing forward, but the apparatus had begun to creak. Her sturdy exterior began to seem insufficient, reduced to its elements: her jewelry, her shiny purse with the loud snap, her gray eyes, all of which had always encompassed and smoothed the rougher edges of the family past. How small she was; how much, thought Lee, this one small person had made in her world, and the worlds of her children.

"This trip is starting to seem really quite mad," she said.

"Don't worry. We'll figure it out."

"Do you think so?"

He put his arm around her and gave her a slight hug. "He hasn't gone anywhere, has he?"

They went on grimly to the fourth place, a down-at-the-heels Methodist church that made Lee's heart sink, the way one feels driving up to a squalid two-family house that was listed by the realtor as a "Victorian gem." They were all—even Richard, who showed the wear and tear of his long night of television—relieved not to find the grave there, but now the situation was becoming desperate. His own pressures were rising: it was eleven-thirty. "Call at twelve," the message from the client had said, a little bastard barely over twenty-five whom Lee had been courting without dignity for months. How Lee would love to blow him off, kiss off the whole thing. New York seemed far enough away to do just that, as if all those bills and all those endless terrors could be simply buried, thrown into a forgotten grave with the old suicide, a fitting place for them both. Closure, as his mother had said. But he had no choice. His mother could remove him from his life for a day or two, pick up all the tabs, and even peel off a few twenties as pocket change, but it wouldn't change anything.

"I've got to call my office," he said casually, hoping to introduce the thought gently. They were waiting for a light to change.

"Really? Can't it wait?"

Lee should have noticed that this was the first time she had ever taken the slightest issue when his work appeared to conflict with other plans, but he did not. "It'll just take a minute. It's important."

She looked at him coldly. "Oh, that feckless work of yours," she said and then started off across the street.

"What do you mean by that?"

She stood in the center, obviously horrified, and very confused, to discover that she had spoken aloud. She began to plead. "I just meant you seem to be able to make your own schedule."

"I'm not going to ask permission to check in with my office," he shouted.

"Of course not," she said. She looked drained.

"I just meant sometime around lunchtime," he said. "Let's check out the last place."

The fifth church on her list was closest to the university and looked big enough to seat two thousand people. The hallways of the "Parish Suite" hummed and churned like an insurance office. Ruth explained their mission, and they were shown to a lounge, with a long table in the center stacked with religious pamphlets and laser-printed testimonials. They waited ten minutes, ten clicks of the watch hand that Lee marked in gathering waves of anxiety. Finally, an ancient church lady came out to tell them she was sorry. The gentleman's earthly remains had not been interred in this churchyard. Lee jumped to his feet, but the woman, speaking in a way that seemed almost pitilessly roundabout to him, continued: Dr. DeLois, the minister, would be out in a moment to help them.

"You go," Ruth said to Lee. "Make your call and we'll meet back at the hotel."

"We'll have lunch," he said, and took his leave. By the

time he had made it back to his room the old dread was back, undiminished by this short vacation. He dialed his office first to see if there had been any further message from the client, and his officemate answered Lee's line with the previously agreed "Nichols Associates, may I help you?" The check had not come. Okay, Lee thought, maybe the Gristede's check will bounce, maybe even his office phone, but the rent must have cleared by now. That was the main thing. And then he made the second call. He was put on hold for five minutes until the client came on the line. "It's a go," he said. "Let's get together and kick it off."

"Great," said Lee. "I'm delighted."

"How about tomorrow morning at ten?"

"Actually, I'm calling from out of town."

There was a pause. "I thought you said your schedule was clear. This is an important project for us."

It wasn't important; it was a goddamned series of sales brochures for mutual funds. It didn't have to start tomorrow; it had been hanging fire for months. The only reason it mattered to anyone in the world was that Lee needed the money and this kid needed to flatter himself by pulling a power play with a freelancer. Was that really what life was about? "I'm here in Hattiesburg, Mississippi, on family business," he said, telling the truth at last.

"We're on the CEO's calendar," said the kid, and that's where it ended, with Lee saying Sure, fine, I'll make it. You can count on me.

. . .

He found his mother and Richard sitting outside the Ramada at a small patio table only a few feet from the traffic. The sight, finally, broke his heart, but he tried to cheer himself and her with a lame joke. "Pay dirt?" he called out.

She beckoned him to sit down. "Some people simply have no manners," she said.

He didn't know who his mother was referring to, but he knew what she meant, not just people being polite and saying thank you, but people caring for others, even for strangers. That's what she meant. "Yeh," he answered. "I know."

"That terrible man, that *Doctor* DeLois, suggested I might be 'confused.' He talked to me like a nursing-home attendant."

For the first time, Lee recognized the possibility that she was indeed wrong about all of this, that her father wasn't buried in Hattiesburg, that her mind was going. "You are sure he's here?"

She reacted, as he expected, with a show of astonishment and hurt. They paused while an enormous truck rolled past them. When it was quiet again she said, "For all I know, my aunt Helen had him exhumed the night they left Hattiesburg, and had his body thrown into the river." She smiled, and then added, "But no. He's here." She reached over and gave Richard a comforting pat; it was the way she liked to change subjects.

But Lee wasn't satisfied. "Isn't this enough closure?

This effort we all made? It doesn't matter whether you find him or not. This trip can be closure. Unless there's more to it."

"I have no secret to divulge, if that's what you think. It's silly, I suppose, but I wanted you to understand my father's mistakes."

"I understand them," Lee answered.

"I have too much time to myself these days," she continued, not really hearing what Lee had said. "I have no discipline over my thoughts. I talk to myself in my bath, and when I realize Frieda can hear me, I pretend I'm talking on the telephone."

"You don't have a telephone in your bathroom, do you? Frieda would know that."

She shrugged. "It came to me last week that the three of us, you and me and Richard, should stand over what remains of that man. I thought he could speak to you, in some way. I thought if we stood on my father's grave, you could see what despair leads to. I'm terrified for you, living such an unconnected life. I don't think you understand how hard you make your life. I want you to get help. I want you to let us help you."

Lee could find no way to react to this statement; he could not thank her for her love, could not get angry at her for underestimating his hold on life. If there were anything easy about these things, he could go over to her and tell her, *Yes, I understand. You don't need to put yourself*

through any more of this. He could take an hour and make
her see that he was not just saying what she wanted to hear,
like the alcoholic saying to his best friend, *Thank you for
showing such concern,* and then heading straight out to a
bar and getting blasted. But no: he had to catch a plane.
Same old Lee, looking for the exit.

"Did you get good news on the phone?" his mother
asked.

He tried to speak, but could not, so much shame in his
life, so many stains. He had to sit, strangled, while she said
it for him. "You have to get back? Is that it?"

"Yes."

She opened her purse, and came up with a plane schedule. He put his hand on hers. "I've already got a reserva-
tion."

"I thought we were going bowling," said Richard. "You
promised."

Lee tried to brush this off with a shrug, but he kept his
attention on his mother. "I didn't have a choice."

"I know, dear. Of course."

There it was: instant forgiveness, smoothing the way on
the road to hell. "You don't mean that," he said.

"No, I don't, but let's drop it. It's the way it is. Richard
and I will stay as we planned." She picked up her compact
and patted her face, and finished by inspecting her bright-
est and most winning smile in the small mirror and then
for another second, as she had always done, a small lifetime

habit, she held the look for her companions, the final inspection. She left the smile there. "Why don't you go wash for lunch," she said to Richard.

Richard nodded, but did not leave the table. Lee had not looked at the boy throughout this, and when he did he saw that Richard's glances were bouncing back and forth between them as if trying to decide who was hurting him, and that he was fighting tears. In that instant Lee received the knowledge that Richard had sat in this wordless way through countless family battles, his father and his mother going at it over the kitchen table. Rick, such an autocratic older brother, a covetous sibling: plenty for a son of any age to figure out. Lee stood up from his chair, pulled the vacant one over closer to the boy, and sat down with his arm landing on Richard's shoulder. Lee could feel the initial tense resistance to this caress, and then the muscles relaxed, and Richard turned his body into Lee's full embrace. The prickly crew-cut head scraped Lee's cheeks like his father's unshaved beard, but he held on.

Two hours later Lee and Richard stood in the Hattiesburg airport. He had said good-bye to his mother in the cab, and she had thanked him for being nice to the boy. It was easy, said Lee. "Maybe this trip has succeeded more than you know," he said. He would have gone on, made promises, blubbered out apologies, but she was past that. She had seen him off plenty of times before and she would do it again.

"How nice. Have a safe trip."

Lee looked around the airport. In place of the families at the train station, the pitch of excitement and the eager anticipation of children for the roll of the locomotives' thunder, he saw only the tired, self-important glaze of the businessman, the one with two-bit accounts.

"I wish I didn't have to go," he said to Richard.

"I had fun last night. Mom wouldn't have let me watch *Terminator 2*." Richard pretended to puff himself up, into an Arnold Schwarzenegger, and it was a funny sight, and an even funnier thought that this sweet boy with the soft middle and thin arms would grow up into something like that. He was trying to cheer Lee up.

"On your next vacation, come to New York and we'll go to every gory movie in town."

"You mean it?"

"Yes," said Lee. "I do."

"Cool!"

"You're a good kid, Richard. You're a great kid."

"Thanks. Uncle Lee. I like you too."

Lee filed into the plane and took his seat at the window. He kept his face firmly plastered against the Plexiglas while they taxied, catching a glimpse of the black dome of the university administration building, and then the higher buildings, plain small boxes and spires, the bland but clean skyscape of a little Southern city that might just be one of the first places in America to show the way out of years of decay. Why couldn't he have stayed? They might have found the grave in an hour or two, and stood at it with a hastily purchased sprig of flowers. Lee pictured the three of them, the ordeal done, standing at the man's tombstone for the moment of silence that anyone—even this man— would deserve, and then heading off to dinner at the Super King Catfish Restaurant and bowling at the Hub City Lanes. He'd remember such an evening fondly for the rest of his life.

He turned quickly as his seatmate's elbow stabbed him in the back. The man was trying to stuff a briefcase and laptop computer under the seat. What a vision. Lee had done this so many times before, confident and smug in his starched shirt and suit, called in from out of town by a client willing to pay any price, shoulder any expense, for his expert services. The hollowness of it. But perhaps by the time he reached Atlanta he'd be over these aches. He'd call Tina while he waited and tell her that he loved her, and hope she wouldn't think he was making a joke. He had a job waiting for him in New York. He would spend all night writing checks, an orgy of repayment, even if he couldn't mail them for a few days. He'd be back in the world, re- deemed and whole, and then maybe that would be the time to make a change.

The plane reached the head of the runway and in a minute or two was banking sharply upwards. Lee kept his eyes on the cold ground, the ground that held his grand- father's remains, discarded by the man's own hand, the ultimate flight. Lee could not speculate on the suicide's anger, but he knew something about the hollowness, about the loneliness of departure, driving away from home gatherings into frosty purple mornings while his mother, and his siblings, and his in-laws slept, a flippant note of good-bye left in front of the toaster.

His seatmate turned to him and asked him what he did, and what his business was in Hattiesburg. Family stuff, said Lee, just family stuff in Hattiesburg. The man rolled his eyes: women and babies, and elderly parents and drunken aunts, and getting hell from your wife. Families. Thank God for the office, huh? Amen. Lee did not correct this unspoken assumption, but watched the man raise his double bourbon as a hopeless toast, or a confession, or perhaps just a lesson for us all.

The Way People Run

Off the road, at least a hundred yards into the yellow scrub, Barry thinks he sees an animal, maybe an antelope, nuzzling the arid brush. He's surprised that it has wandered so far out into the open, alone. About a mile ahead he sees the town, or what's left of it— a few blanched hackberry skeletons above a small gathering of houses centered on a two-story brick block. Even from this distance, he can tell that the wooden cornices and pediments of this structure, the Commerce Building, are rotting. He has been seeing buildings like these and towns like this one for days, out here on the Plains; the only way he has of knowing that there are any people left is the sizzling rays of neon beer signs from one or two of the windows in an otherwise shuttered facade. He glances at his speedometer, and then back at the antelope, but what he first saw as an animal in the brush has broken apart, exploded limb by limb into children, six or seven of them suddenly scattered from their clustered spot. They are all different sizes, and as they run, one of the big ones tugs along the littlest, a girl three or four years old, not much smaller than his daughter, if the distance, and the shafts of morning light through the rain heads, and Barry's tired eyes can be trusted.

The café in town is still called the Virginian. Barry walks into the darkness, not sure if it will hold him. The place smells of cigarettes and beer—not such a bad combination if left to age on its own, but the air is sugary with air freshener. Lilac, maybe, or Mountain Meadow. Someone is keeping a business going in here, perhaps because the county road crew stops in three times a week, or because the motor vehicle department opens a desk at one of the tables once a quarter. The tables around the edge of the room are dull black squares rimmed with the semicircles of Windsor chairs. The lamplight is bloodied by red shades at the tables and the bar, but in the center of the room, dominating the territory encompassed by its brilliant processed fluorescence, is a circular pie cabinet. It is steel and glass and looks so new that Barry wonders if it is for sale. On the third of six carousel shelves there is an apple pie, scarred by the removal of a single triangle, revolving in solitary repetition.

Barry assumes that the Virginian survives partly on the whims of strangers, but the waitress greets him with a surprised glance anyway. He looks for a name tag, or a hint that she might be a relative of his. She's about his age, forties, sharp-jawed, and very thin, so thin in her tight blue jeans that she looks almost sexless. She shows him to a table and sets up the silverware in front of him. He sees the pie revolving, watches it several times, and then moves to the chair that faces the wall. When the waitress comes back with his menu she stares hard enough at his emptied place to force him to explain.

"That pie thing," Barry says. "It's sort of distracting." It's possible that she will find this funny.

The waitress looks at him neutrally, which seems almost a favor. She's not going to knock the establishment; it's clear she's got the only job in town.

"Why is this place called the Virginian?" he asks, looking up from his menu. He has always wondered if the café was named after the book.

She shrugs. "Can't say. Is that where you're from?"

He shakes his head. He hopes she won't ask "Where, then?" because the true answer is "New York." He hopes she won't ask "So what line are you in?" because these days he's not in any line at all, just sort of looking for work.

"Tourists don't stop in here much," she offers.

"Well, no, but . . ."

But what? Coming out West hadn't made a whole lot of sense from the beginning. Barry had started this trip with interviews in Los Angeles—fund management, trading, stockbroking, anything with money—even though no one suggested there were any jobs there. He had a briefcase full of recommendations, résumés that came flooding out of copiers and laser printers by the ream in the last days of his firm on Wall Street. At first he called home every night to report. At each stop in California he kept hearing of the boom in Washington state—Boeing and Microsoft—and he became part of a wave of suppliants heading north, pilgrims in business suits trying hard not to recognize each other from earlier waiting rooms. He began to want anything that wasn't his: someone's job, someone's car, someone's family. He hit bottom one night in a Seattle hotel that was far shabbier than he ought to have risked, considering his mood. He canceled his last interview and headed back over the Cascades toward home, but in the desert he began to lose his way. He was not entirely sure how many days he had been gone. The hundred-dollar bills that he had watched closely and had broken with extreme anxiety now seemed endless, sufficient forever. An obscure elation began to take the place of schedule and plan. And then, as if planted in his mind like a signpost, came the image of this town, and he turned south for it even as his wife, Polly, wailed on the telephone, as she demanded to know what this detour could possibly do to relieve their plight.

The waitress loses interest during this pause and backs off; she's not going to hazard any piece of herself with him, and there's no reason for her to. "What can I get you?" she asks.

Barry looks at his watch and tries to recall the last three or four times he's eaten, decides it's time for a full midday meal, and orders a strip steak. "Our mashed potatoes are real," says the menu. It has begun to seem almost miraculous that he can stop in these ruined Western towns and find food; it's been days since he's seen cattle, or fields of corn, or vegetable gardens; he doesn't even see delivery trucks on the road. He's been asking waitresses, "Do you still have any bacon?" or "What have you got?" as if menus were just memories of the times before a civil war out there cut off supplies. He feels the same way about gas; he's begun to feel the same way about women.

Barry hears the voices of two men behind him—he saw them under their feed-store caps at the bar when he walked in—and suddenly he regrets turning his back on the room. Each time he overhears a conversation he feels he has made a connection with a new place; in the same way, it reassures him to read notices for upcoming county fairs and church events, as if he will still be there when the date rolls around. The waitress is going to think he's crazy, he knows, but finally he can't resist the men at the bar, so he moves to a third side of the table.

"Maybe I should put it here and wait for you to catch up to it," she says when she returns, holding his plate above the fourth place. She gives him a smile somewhere between exasperation and interest.

"No. I'm settled now," says Barry. He says this straight, unthinkingly, as part of this conversation, but the statement taken in its own slender context is ridiculous, so ridiculous that he finishes it with a kind of bleating laugh on the "now."

A little off, the waitress seems to decide; he's okay but just a little off. She puts down his plate and does not wait to ask him how everything is. He thinks it might be funny to ask her for fresh-ground pepper.

The food is quite good, and he relaxes as he eats. The café's rusting tin ceiling is high above him. Above that ceiling, on the second floor, there were once rooms to let, and in one of those rooms his mother spent a week or two just after the war. Barry can imagine the sounds she heard from the other rooms, lovemaking and the beribboned serenade of a Bakelite Motorola. The country was flooding then, filling with expectation, and she had gone in the moment of this triumph to the Plains to find her father, his grandfather, who had, so long ago, lost heart. The story of their meeting and the final hurt it had caused her had become over the years, for Barry and his sisters, the text for a sort of catechism: What is the true nature of man? How does sin have power over the weakest of us? What is meant by betrayal of all things proper and holy? Barry pictures his mother, her clothes neatly placed in the dresser, her pearls and her aspirin arranged on a stained white table furrowed with cigarette burns.

The waitress is sitting behind the cash register, reading

a fashion magazine in the light of the pie cabinet. He beckons to her for another beer. She remembers that he is drinking Olympias, and he feels rooted in her recognition, and when she brings it to him, in fact, she lingers. The men at the bar have left.

"When I was coming in I thought I saw children out on the plain," he says.

"I expect you did," she says. "Probably dropping cherry bombs down gopher holes."

"Isn't there a school here?" he asks, thinking of Polly's checklist for evaluating any town they might move to: good schools, health care, Episcopal or Presbyterian church, pretty streets, Victorian houses, a Toyota dealership.

"In Rylla. But the bus has been broke for a couple of days." She picks up his plate and asks, "You want a piece of pie?"

Barry asks her for the check instead. He's ready to find out if she had known his grandfather. Back on the street he blinks in the sun; the clouds have passed and now there's no color to the light, just illumination, just the searing pressure of day on these powdery buildings. He opens a road map on the hood of his car and then stares over it. There is a white church building with a yard bounded by rusty sheep fencing; the church had once been repainted up to about five feet high all around, and it looks as if it is sinking. Beside the church is a brown house trailer with two bicycles in front, and then a low green ranch with flowers in the yard, and finally an old gas station with an enigmatic hand-painted sign running like bunting across the windows and door, saying WELCOME TO ELEVEN-MILE RODEO. The old man had been happy here; that was his chief offense, the irreparable rebuke carried home by his daughter, and the principal evidence of his madness.

"You lost?"

Barry looks up and sees the waitress blinking at him. He thinks for a moment that she is making a joke. "Which way to Broadway," he asks.

"You ain't there," she says, but she doesn't laugh. Place, her place, isn't funny to her.

He thinks of the biggest city around and tells her that's where he's going.

"I go up there to the dentist," she says. She has nice teeth, maybe a little too big for her mouth, but they are straight and white. There are some bills from the orthodontists awaiting him at home.

He folds up the map and sees her noticing the pile of maps, maybe a hundred of them, which are spilled out onto the passenger seat of his car. This is how it has been lately: catching a glimpse of himself through other eyes. He can't help what they perceive, but he has been careful to shave regularly.

"You know," Barry says, "I've been wanting to ask you. I had some relatives who lived here once."

"Is that so?" She's at least somewhat interested in this unexpected fact, but not enough to ask who, as Barry thought she certainly would.

"Actually, it was my grandfather. Gordon Fox." Barry does not want to admit that he does not know when or how the old man died. Barry's mother must have killed her father off in a hundred different speculations, all of them deserved, asked for: drunken staggerings into danger, truculent exposures to the rages of others.

"You're kidding," the waitress says. She whistles. "Old Gordon!"

Barry looks at her carefully to gauge the reaction; claiming kinship with this maligned man could yield unpredictable results.

"Well, I'll be damned," she says, affectionately. She's smiling, at last, and it's quite a nice smile; it fills out her thin face and makes her softer. "He was a funny old prairie dog. He sort of collected cars. You ought to see his place." She gives him quick directions; out here, all directions are quick, even if the distances are long.

He shrugs as if this whole matter were actually not why he came, as if he had business to get on with, and she walks away. He watches her disappear around the church toward the edge of town. He gets in his car and backs out between a dusty Ford pickup and a Subaru; he thinks for a moment that they aren't real vehicles, just junkers without engines that have been left there by the owner of the Virginian to make the place seem popular. He gets back onto the main road, and then turns in the direction she told him, back the way he came. He makes a few notations for his journal on the dashboard notepad. These days the journal is nothing but weather; he had recently kept pace with a front, going seventy to remain in the wind and black light, for hundreds of miles. It had left him breathless and exhilarated, as if he had been sailing in a gale.

Back on the prairie the children are one again; Barry imagines the pattern of their clusters and star-shaped explosions across the flats as fireworks. He keeps glancing over at them, and suddenly one of them breaks off and seems to be dancing madly around—a kind of Indian game, maybe. Barry looks again, and this time it seems that what is happening is that the child is waving at him, that they are all waving at him now. He stops the car and peers over; they are yelling at him. He gets out and begins walking toward them; the soil and dry fuzz of undergrowth are brittle; his footsteps crunch like broken glass. A little way out he recognizes that he has underestimated the distance. It gets hot, and he slips off his Shetland sweater.

When Barry begins to close in on the children they turn back away from him, all looking at something at their feet. Now that he is drawing within several yards he realizes that it is one of the children on the ground. The boy has both his hands pressed white against his left eye socket. There is a little blood on his cheek and forehead and even some coming through his fingers. When Barry sees this he leaps forward. "What happened. What happened?" he says. "Is he all right?"

There are mumbles, but no one answers, not even the biggest, who must be at least sixteen. Instead, they just stare down at the damaged creature curled at their feet. There's a white dusting of soil on his hair and clothes. Barry kneels and says to the boy, "What's hurt? Are you okay?"

"My eye," the boy says, scared but not crying. The little girl, the one Barry had noticed earlier from the car, is whimpering, but the rest are silent.

"Jesus," says Barry. "Let's see." He reaches out and takes hold of one of the skinny wrists. The boy fights him, and Barry isn't sure what he is doing is right, because maybe the boy is really holding the eye in his head like this; maybe, all things considered, keeping pressure on it is best.

"What happened?" Barry says one more time, this time directing the question at the oldest.

"Firecracker must of lifted a rock or something. Didn't see it hit."

Barry looks at the firecrackers on the ground, and they seem big enough to be dynamite; they aren't what he would have called cherry bombs.

"Has someone gone to get help?" No one says anything; they are helpless and hopeless. Barry lets go of the boy's wrist, gently pressing his hand to tell him that he has changed his mind, that he doesn't want to see the wound, that it will be best to keep the pressure on. Barry steadies himself on his knees and then lets fly at the entire group of them: What did you idiots *think* was going to happen? Why aren't you in school. This is the stupidest thing I've ever heard of. Why do your parents allow you to do this?

This long outburst has no effect on the children, but it calms Barry, makes him feel that he is acting suitably parental. Now that this is established, he picks up the boy in his arms. The load is lighter than he expected, but they're a long way out; his car seems very distant. "Go ahead and tell someone to get a doctor," he shouts angrily at the others. They leave in a pack and head out for town.

Barry is alone with the injured child. "What's your name?" he asks, trying not to sound winded.

The boy snuffles. Barry has to stop for a moment to take the weight off his arms by crouching over his knees. "You're hurting me," says the boy.

The boy smells musty, almost sour, nothing like the limpid fragrance of Barry's son and daughter. The child's hair is coarse and spiky, and his twin cowlicks rub Barry's arm raw; the boy's mouth is open, and Barry can see a gray spot of decay on one of his crooked teeth. The boy is becoming almost repellent to him, with these unexpressed needs and sullenly accepted salvation, as if what the others knew was that this child deserved this missile in his eye, that it was his fault. Barry wishes the boy would cry or whimper or call out; this wounded silence, as if life or sight did not matter, is perhaps the worst of it.

"Just a little way to go now," says Barry. He's hoping that by the time he gets back to the road someone from the town will have come; he doesn't want to get blood on Polly's Camry, though that's not going to keep him from doing the right thing. But no one is there, so he bats away the piles of maps on the passenger seat and lays the boy there. He goes out into the grasses and tries to rub some of the hardening blood from his hands.

Barry looks out for a car coming the other way, but there is nothing on the road; he's driving carefully to keep the boy from dropping his head onto the door upholstery. He has begun to fear that the boy and his dripping eye have been ceded to him for good, no take-backs. But there is, finally, some activity in town; a woman comes streaming out of the green ranch as he rounds the corner, and another woman and a younger man are climbing into a truck, a cherry-red Ford pickup with chrome pipes and reflective windows. The truck is so immaculate that Barry wonders how it got here; it's like an ocean liner on a lake. Barry expects to see the waitress; for some reason he has assumed all along that she will be the first person he greets, that the boy might even be hers.

"Wendell," yells the woman in the truck. She's a sight for this town—almost punk, with lots of makeup and a black leather jacket.

The boy still doesn't cry. What's wrong with him? Barry

thinks. He's like a fish that seems to feel nothing as a hook is yanked from its throat.

The woman pulls the car door open and helps the boy out. "Can you see through it?"

"I dunno," the child says.

This single answer changes the woman's tone. "You know to stand clear," she says harshly, giving him a shake. She's treating him now as if he were a careless construction worker. "Get in the truck and we'll take you to the doctor."

"No," the boy says, and finally, after all this, he begins to wail. It's the doctor and the waiting room, the smell of pain and the glint of needles, that set him off. Thank God, thinks Barry, the kid's human. In a few moments they are off, with not a word to Barry. He thinks suddenly—it comes with the visual force of hallucination—that this town is someone's miniature, exposed from above. He looks into the sky and expects to see an enormous moon-eyed face blotting out the sun.

He's weaving on the sidewalk when this vision passes, and he looks up in surprise to see the little girl standing in front of him, her overall straps loose on her tiny arms. She's dirt-streaked and is holding a filthy pink blanket with tattered strips of satin binding, but her hair is perfect under two purple barrettes.

"The boy's going to be all right," Barry calls out. "Wendell is going to be fine." He doesn't know why he says this, except that whenever something frightening or bad happens around Mike and Pattie, he tells them that it will be all right. He tells them this even as he sinks into despair. Four children killed by stray bullets in a single night, they hear on the radio, and Dad says, "It's all right. They're in heaven."

The girl asks, "Are you in the army?"

"No," Barry responds, not unfamiliar with the abruptness of a four-year-old's conversation.

"Will you play with me for these many minutes?" The girl holds up a sticky palm with all five digits spread.

"How many is that?" Barry asks encouragingly.

"Eight."

A voice comes from across the street just as Barry is ready to smile. "Winona! Don't talk to that man. Come here."

Barry figures the woman is just a little paranoid, and tries not to take it personally; he is a stranger, even if he did just save the life or eye or something of one of this town's sons. "That's right," he says to the girl. "Don't talk to strangers."

"Winona!"

The girl hesitates just long enough to exert a measure of defiance; she knows what Barry said to them out on the prairie was right. The girl, he sees now in a flash, is responding to discipline as the books say: They like it because it puts order in their lives and shows them grown-ups care. But the mother has got another lesson in mind, and she runs over to the girl and belts her. Then she grabs her as if yanking her out of the way of an oncoming tractor trailer and retreats. The mother and daughter reach the other side again, and the woman turns to defy him straight on, large breasts pushed out like musculature. When she's satisfied Barry has been warned away sufficiently, she pulls the little girl back into the house. Barry sees then that what he took for flowers in her yard is actually litter: waxed cardboard from frozen vegetable packs, tufts of white tissue, the orange spiral from a box of Tide.

Barry stands there flushed with anger. He cannot imagine how he could be treated as dangerous to small children by this person who allows a toddler to play with explosives. Kids are one thing Barry knows. Everyone says he is great with kids. He cannot deny that he's a little uninvolved with his own children's daily experiences—Polly's a superb mother, really quite remarkable—but he's always figured that they feel he cares. They'll grow up with the confidence that they were loved by both parents. That's what he has assumed.

Barry is getting more and more indignant as he climbs back into his car; he's *from* this town, for God's sake. Sort of. He heads into the prairie. He thinks back to the directions the waitress gave him to his grandfather's spread: Go west and go left. He likes the sound of it; he relaxes his anger and makes himself laugh heartily at the thought of those directions becoming some sort of credo for his grandfather, something for his family crest.

Barry's mother's campaign to eradicate her father's memory had been so meticulous and so persistent that there was virtually nothing about his grandfather's flight that Barry did not know. It began in 1930 with an empty place at the head of the dinner table in Hartford, a setting of china and silverware removed by the maid halfway through soup. Lobster bisque, if Barry recalled correctly. He had always been quite fond of his grandmother, a gutsy lady, and had suspected that her life had been full and happy since her husband split. But for years, dutifully, Barry had taken his mother's side in this matter, and even now, a pilgrim to the man's final place of rest, Barry can't imagine him being called, affectionately, "a funny old prairie dog."

He comes to a gravel road, about one mile beyond the point where he had found the children, and takes a left. The wheel tracks are deep as wagon trails, and the grass and brush bend under the car. He drives slowly, up over one rise and down into a deep broad basin. He seems not to be getting anywhere, for all this motion; the land just keeps rising and falling endlessly.

He drives on, and is finally aware of a different quality in the light behind the next rise, strands of luminescence. He reaches the crest and is immediately dazzled by a thousand shards of sun. Then, as his eyes adjust, he sees the source of all this confused display. He understands what the wait-ress meant when she said the old man collected cars. There are hundreds of them following the contours of the bowl, automobiles and vehicles of other sorts, things on wheels of every possible type. The sun finds the untarnished sur-faces on all of them—chrome bumpers, headlamps and rearview mirrors, hoods still lustrous, and metallic-flaked fenders. The place is spotless and beautiful, as beautiful as anything he has seen on this trip through unrelieved decay and decline. Barry is stunned and uplifted by this dreadful vision. It could be nothing but a junkyard, but the man was clearly up to something, and whether or not he thought of it this way, he left behind a monument.

Barry gets out of his car and sits, watching the sun mark an hour or two on the face of this immense obsession. He tries hard, with as much concentration as he has put on anything in the past few months, to figure out what it means. He has not felt so refreshed in many days, has not sensed so many options since he was a teenager. There are invitations on the tip of every blade of grass.

After a while, the rush passes. If there was a sign for him here, he has not found it, or he has not divined its mean-ing. Perhaps he has made a mistake coming here after all.

There is no one in the Virginian. Barry grabs a newspa-per—it's a few days old—and feels bold enough to go over to his table against the back wall and crack open the storm shutter. A shaft of white light cuts out a wedge on the greasy surface. He unfolds his paper and reads about high school sports, and then the social news. At one point a man comes in and walks straight to the bar and draws himself a draught beer with all the familiarity of someone getting water from his kitchen sink; he stands for a moment, gives Barry a canine scowl over the rim of his glass, finishes the beer and then slaps a handful of change on the bar before leaving. The bartender returns an hour or two later, sees the money and drops it, coin by coin, into the separate bins of his cash register. It doesn't sound like much of a gross receipt for a long afternoon, and in fact, the bartender glares at Barry, as if he damn well could have contributed something himself.

Barry goes back to his paper, and in a few more minutes the door opens and the waitress comes in. He is gratified by the strong nod of recognition he gets, and is positively flattered when she walks directly to his table. She's wearing a name tag now, pinned to her gray sweater—something more formal for supper, perhaps, or a way of introducing herself to him, maybe. Her name is May. "That was you. You brought Wendell Peters in."

Barry had forgotten, for these few moments, about the boy, and the modest surprise he shows is genuine. "Oh, that! Yes, I guess I did. Quite a thing."

"I can't believe it." She's very upset.

"How is he?"

"You don't know?"

"What?" he asks. How could he know anything. He could have been two hundred miles away by now.

"He's going to lose the eye. They're taking it out right now up at Good Shepherd." She turns to blow her nose.

Barry believes this; the boy was too still and didn't cry. Their pediatrician had always made a joke about that: "The louder they cry . . ." He thinks of the boy's almost rancid odor. The feeling of the spiky hair comes back, and with it Barry's recognition that he had been hoping for something dramatic out of this, something more than a few stitches in the boy's eyebrow. "It didn't seem that bad," Barry says, defending himself against his thoughts.

"I told them it was dangerous," says May.

Barry reflects that she had not sounded alarmed or nervous at lunch when she described to him what the children were doing. "Of course you did. My son is a real hell-raiser. Never listens," he adds, trying to remember whether he had told her before that he was a parent. He's been doing a good bit of lying out here—things like pretending he served in Vietnam, during Tet or in the Delta, or saying that he grew up in Arizona—harmless lies, just to ease his way among strangers.

May smiles, finally. "My boy, Everett, is so cautious he scares himself when he sneezes. He's six," she adds.

Wendell, Everett, Winona. What's with the names in this town? he wonders. "So he wasn't there?"

She seems slightly insulted by this deduction. "Well, sure he was there." She wrings a dishtowel that she has been holding the whole time. "It gives me shivers." She produces a real shiver, a trembling in her shoulders, and when it is done she asks, "Do you want a beer, an Oly?"

Barry nods, feeling utterly, extravagantly at home. He has never had a regular eating place, or a regular bar, and has never felt like a patron of any establishment, except for the paper stand at the mouth of his subway stop. But in this one day he has started to act as if he owned this table, and the people who have been drifting into the bar seem to expect to see him sitting there. He feels a permanence, as if the accidents of the day could not have occurred with a mere passerby. He likes May. Besides, he has been watching her thin-hipped body and is very turned on by her. He has never been unfaithful to Polly, but this could be different—physical and free. His saliva becomes electric at the hard-core images in his mind.

May brings him a beer and then recommends he order the pork chops. "Sure," he says.

Suddenly the door to the Virginian bursts open, and Barry recognizes the man who served himself at the bar earlier. He wavers in the doorway and then appears to remind himself to shout out hysterically. "They saved it! They think they saved the eye!"

There is a moment of reduced conversational hum. The man is obviously Wendell's father, quite a bit older than the wife who had claimed Wendell earlier and driven off with a younger man. "That's good, Frank," says one male voice, but it is followed by a few snickers. It turns out that the medical report is the product of one drunk's self-serving imagination. Frank weaves slightly but holds his place, as if he still expects to be mobbed at the door and carried aloft to the bar for a celebration. At last, May takes the man's hand and leads him over. The bartender shares a look with May, and then pours half a draught beer.

Barry himself is drinking more tonight than he has for weeks, months; he lost the taste for it just about the time depression took away all his other pleasures: sex, food, tennis. May brings his supper, and then checks back with him in the course of the evening, bringing him beers, giving him the quick line on the other customers, almost all of them men. There's not much else to do here. One of the drunks yells at May to get her "skinny ass over here," and he tries to goose her when she walks by. Barry knows he must accept the fact that she could not possibly have any interest in spending time with him. However this woman lives her life, it won't be him she's sleeping with tonight. He is beginning to crash, falling back on nothing but the foul breath of his night's drinking. He thinks about unrolling his sleeping bag and starts to look forward with dread to the morning's wet dew.

"Where are you staying?" asks May. It's now just about closing time, and he's one of the last people left in the Virginian. The man who grabbed her has gone. "Going to Rylla or something?"

Barry says, "Sure." Maybe that's it, a motel in Rylla.

"Well, you know," she says.

Barry reads May's hooded, apologetic eyes and slightly set lips, and is stunned to realize that all his unspoken prayers have been answered. She's going to ask him to stay—if not with her, then at least at her place. And she does.

"I've got a spare bedroom."

He accepts. She goes about her clean-up duties, and she makes no attempt at all to hide him; there's nothing furtive here, nothing to apologize for, as if everyone in the room would wish her well in finding a little unexpected companionship.

The air in May's house—one of two small bungalows behind the church—is stuffy with the chemical odors of carpeting. Most of the living room is taken up with a wooden-armed Colonial sofa, covered with a print of New England village scenes. The lamps and shades are part of the same set, and everything is very neat; the walls and the ceiling are the same unfortunate light green. A man hasn't lived here in a long time—maybe never. There is a collection of china farm animals on a small hanging bookshelf. Barry pictures her adding to this collection, buying a new piece in Rylla and carrying it home in a box of cotton, taking it out and finding the best place for it on the shelf beside the other knickknacks. He sits on the sofa, following her with his ears as she wakes her boy, carries him to the toilet so he can pee, returns him to bed, and begins to make coffee in the kitchen. There seems to have been no baby-sitter. Barry tries to figure out where the spare bedroom must be.

May talks to him from the kitchen—a confident intimacy, as if he is always where she expects him to be, even if she can't see him. "You know, I'm still real skittish about that accident. Poor Wendell."

Barry yells back, "Yeah, there's something really frightening about an eye injury. Eyes seem so vulnerable anyway."

She is obviously so struck by the aptness of this comment that she leans her head around the door to answer. "That's a real interesting point."

Barry is quite amazed that he is doing so well; it really has been some time since he's tried to converse. "Eyes are so important," he says in a loud whisper, now that she has returned to the stove. There is a clinking of mugs and the rattle of a burner grate on a range.

Barry scouts around the room, looking at the tabletops and the shallow window wells; except for the telephone book, there isn't a single printed word in the house, as far as he can tell. He finds that comforting. "This is very kind of you," he yells again. "This is a very nice home." He's learned in his travels to use the word "home" and not "house," to say "sack" for "paper bag," and to pump his own gas without paying first.

She comes in with the coffee and looks around the room, and it's clear that she, too, is comforted by what she sees. "I like things to be nice," she says. She's relaxed in her private place; he thinks of his wife, Polly. He is upset, but then relieved to find that he can't, at this moment, recall her face.

May shakes him out of his thoughts; he must have been quiet for a beat too long.

"I guess at noontime when you drove in you never thought you'd get involved in something like this," she says.

He isn't sure what she means by "this": her or the town. "You never know."

"It's not always exciting around here." She begins this statement quite straight, but realizes halfway through that it's funny.

"How can you stand all this fun?" says Barry, and they both laugh. He hasn't used irony in weeks; at home, everything that everyone—his friends, people at work, Polly—says is indirect. May eyes him as if she has just realized he has been holding out on her; that he's been playing possum behind all his Eastern reserve. He can tell the idea of making love to him is in her mind.

"Have you ever thought of leaving here?" he asks.

She's already told him she grew up on the other side of the Commerce Building, in a house that burned down. She shakes her head and shrugs at the same time. "It ain't the bright lights," she says, suddenly undreamy and unchildlike and very defensive, "but it's home."

Barry is busy slamming on the brakes. "Sure. You don't understand. I love it here."

"Mom?" It's Everett, his voice just as fearful and squeaky as May made him sound in the café.

"Sh-h-h," says May to Barry, and she crouches as if she were ducking the snare in her son's call.

"Mom? Who's there?"

She gives up. "No one, honey. Go to sleep."

The boy starts to cry—not an entirely convincing cry, to Barry's trained ear. "I had a nightmare. I dreamed grachity was letting go and we all started to float."

May looks at Barry, an apology, and leaves him. When she comes back, after a longer interval than Barry anticipated, she is holding clean, folded sheets, a pillow, and a towel—not a good sign. His heart sinks. But she sits down beside him and puts her foot up on the sofa between them, close enough to touch him, and after a few silent minutes he drops his hand onto her calf. They talk, and then lean forward and kiss. Her saliva has a slightly odd taste and her mouth feels very different from Polly's; her back is hard and taut to his touch, but maybe she's just tense. They move to her bedroom, which is arranged just like a motel room, a low dresser with a mirror above it along the wall opposite the bed. They start to unbutton and unzip each other's clothes, with a few nervous laughs, and then she pulls herself away to the bathroom in disarray. Barry catches sight of his reflection for a moment, and tells his disbelieving and wildly thrilled image that in a very few minutes it will be happening; he will plunge over one of the edges of his life with Polly. He wonders what it would be like to think of it as his "former" life.

May comes back in a pink terry-cloth bathrobe, and it opens, at one point, right up to her waist. She turns out the light and slows things down, making him hold her in his arms for a few minutes in the darkness. Barry is startled by how good this feels—the pressure and heated silk of another's flesh. He has not had sex—or "made love," or whatever he should call this—in some weeks and his stomach churns with desire; his ears seem to ring when, finally, she brushes him. She has almost no buttocks, and her stomach is as flat as a teenager's. He finds softness here and there on her body. When he enters her she feels athletic, wiry as a runner, and she moves in pleasure. It makes him think of Polly's fuller, more cushioned body, inertly receiving, but it ends with a long, almost sweet, chirping from May, and his own surprised thank-yous.

Barry wakes up in the spare bedroom and looks out the window at the early morning. He's looking directly into a cemetery, close enough to read the names on many of the stones, to see the carved image of Calvary etched in the pink granite of the most recent tombstone. Beyond the barbed boundaries of this slightly green plot the yellow plains stretch out to a bare, purple rise. The events of the previous day run quickly past his eyes—the first sight of town, meeting May, the boy's eye, his grandfather's cars; as recent as they are, Barry has the sensation that these random events have been awaiting him for many years. He looks at the life-sized poured-concrete statue of Jesus Christ in the center of the graveyard. It stands on a pedestal of rust-colored concrete marked with the phrase "I Am the Life" arranged in a triangle of letters, a word to a line.

He dresses with as little sound as possible, not because he wants to slip out but because he hears the boy out there. Soon there is a bustle of a child being sent to school, and a door closing—presumably the bus is working again and the town's next generation will not be allowed to play games with explosives. Barry comes out at last. May is still in her bathrobe, and any embarrassment in this meeting is dispelled in a moment. The kitchen's aluminum-legged table is set with two chairs, May's and Everett's. On the cramped counter behind her is a large school portrait of the boy—he's nice looking, with a very slender face—and Barry is relieved at not recognizing him from the roadside. He doesn't believe Everett was out there yesterday.

"You seem real rested," May says. It's clear she thinks it's due to sex with her—and it is, in some part.

"Best I've felt in weeks."

"I slept pretty well myself," she says. She reaches back to rub her neck languidly.

"I like it here a lot," he says. He's sitting in Everett's chair. "I mean the land around here."

"Not much like home," she offers, although Barry doesn't recall telling her where home is. She assumes a position in front of the stove, waiting for his breakfast request.

"I can't explain it, but I feel there are answers here, on your plains. Do you know what I mean?"

She doesn't, really. She has turned her back to the stove and is now facing him.

"It may be a kind of unique place."

Her expression darkens slightly as he tells her that the statue in the cemetery reminded him that Christ went out into the wilderness. "Forty days and forty nights," he hums, trying to get the melody of an old hymn.

"I wouldn't know," she says. "I'm not up on my Bible."

"Neither am I," he admits. This conversation is not going at all well. May is a little unnerved; he can see that much.

She says, "When you're back with your wife and working at your new job you'll think of us, maybe. And Old Gordon's cars."

"I guess," he says. "But I think I'm going to stick around a little longer." Maybe it's time for him to admit—to himself, anyway—that he has left Polly and the kids for good, that he is never going back.

May rewraps her terry cloth tightly across her front and cinches down the cord. "Here?"

"Well, I don't mean freeloading off you."

"Hey," she says. "I like it. You just make it sound a little permanent."

"I just mean I'd like to look around. Maybe see what's possible in real estate."

"Here?" she asks again.

"Pretty crazy, isn't it?"

"I just don't understand. You mean *move* here? Why would anyone *do* that?"

Barry is losing the clarity somewhat. "I'm married," he says. "I have children." He doesn't know why he is telling her this again, after the night before, but it *is* a reason. Isn't it? "Hell," says Barry. He means—and she clearly understands him to mean—that anything is possible in this world. "I'm looking for investment possibilities."

"Not here," May says. "Not in my town. I didn't invite you to stay with me because I was looking for new neighbors."

"I can't ask you to understand. Like Old Gordon," he says, but immediately realizes that mentioning him was a very bad move.

Now she's simply trying to get him out the door. "We had a nice time, a really nice time, but shouldn't you go back East? There's nothing for you here."

"Maybe you have to come from the outside."

"Well," she says. She shrugs. "This whole damn county, this whole damn state, is going down the tubes. You'd have to be nuts . . ." Her thought trails off. Barry can't debate with her. In fact, he's starting to feel quite nonplussed and annoyed by what she is saying: his chest tightens, which is exactly what happens when he's on the telephone with Polly. Being alone, after all, means you can think your own thoughts without interference.

She goes to the sink to do dishes; he never even got a cup of coffee. He thinks of her body inside the bathrobe and wishes they could make love again. It could still happen; if he shows up at her door at ten tonight, she may tell him she's glad he hasn't left yet, that she hopes he'll stay a little longer. She'll be whipping off her clothes as she says this. Or maybe during the day she'll think of him, almost expecting, wanting, him to come back, but he'll be hundreds of miles away by then.

This morning, however, the time is past. He's said or done something a little weird—not that he knows exactly what it is. Now that everything is settled, now that she believes she will never see him again, she can afford to be cheerful. "You going out to see your granddad's place again on your way out? You sure seemed impressed."

He remembers that he carried on a bit about it after they were done with lovemaking. He doesn't answer, wondering if he should be angry about any of this, about May's sleeping with him and then throwing him out, about his grandfather's having left no message or sign for him but a field full of junked cars, about Polly, a thin reed on the end of a telephone line, charting his decline like a stockbroker hoping to find his fifty-two-week low.

"Quite a place," says May. She's still referring to Gordon's fields.

May sees him out the door. A reddish sun is rising over a very cold morning. Barry walks down the dusty path by the church and comes out facing the middle of the Commerce Building. He can see a sign, an incongruously cute rebus, in one of the empty storefronts: FRED AND ALICE'S USED ❋-4 STORE. Quite a place, he thinks as he throws his toilet kit into the trunk of his car. He fishes for a map, not one for a specific state but the one he rarely uses: the western half of the country, from the Mississippi to the Pacific. It spreads out across the dashboard and fills the entire windshield. Thousands of shattered, ruined towns—pulses of light in his own darkened sky.

He turns, finally, for Rylla. It's west, and the sun pushes down from behind. Two or three miles out of town he makes out a large shape on the side of the road. It's the school bus, the town's bus, and he assumes it has broken down again: the front door, the emergency exit, and the hood are all standing open. As he draws close he sees no sign of the children and it's real spooky, as if the bus has been waylaid. He gets out of his car and calls, but there is no answer. He pokes his head in the doorway of the bus and calls again. The key is in the ignition, and on impulse he tries it, but the engine doesn't catch. He knows perfectly well that none of this is his business, and he is about to turn his back when he notices the end of a pink blanket peeping out into the aisle of haze-gray seats. He walks back and picks it up, recognizing it as the beloved and trusted friend of that little girl, Winona. For a moment his mind floods with images—ankle socks, size-six T-shirts, dolls, and vinyl purses shiny with sequins. He quickly drops the blanket and backs out the door into the prairie, and stands there surveying the bounds of this vast, ownerless domain, wondering if this is really the way these things happen, the way people run.

Things Left Undone

On the morning his son was born, Denny McCready walked out to the banks of the Chesapeake to see the dawn. As a farmer does on his endless spirals, lost in meditation to the tractor's unwavering drone, he had been picturing and repicturing this moment for some months as his own special celebration, a complete joy making its own music in the background. Just as he had imagined, the first yellow light dappling the water was full of promise; he could breathe in the textured Bay air and smell the sharp fragrance of the honeysuckle growing along the fence lines behind him. But his heart was not suddenly filled with the majesty of it all. He looked down at his stained hands, resting without task at his side, and they reminded him of season after season, drought followed by too much rain, sickness and health. He took one last glance across the water to Hail Point, a fragile stand of loblolly pines slowly being undermined by the tides and storms, and then he turned, feeling almost as if his love had been found insufficient even as his son was still wet from his first reach lifeward.

Denny began to feel better when he settled in on the telephone, working through the list of friends and family that Susan had prepared weeks ago. On his way through the farmyard he had stopped by the milking parlor, found his father and the hired man, and received a round of congratulations, pats on the back. The baby was named Charles after Denny's father. The sun-creased scowl on the old man's face relaxed for a time into a smoother reflection of satisfaction: it was right for a man to have children, and grandchildren, just as it was right for a farmer to have a dog. The moment was over fairly quickly—it was time to move the milkers to the cows on the other aisle—but as Denny left the others to their labors, he looked back with the sensation that these familiar routines were no longer his, that his life had now slipped slightly out of his control.

A few hours later, showered and shaved, he was back at the hospital. Susan's eyes showed black rings of fatigue, but she had demanded the baby and he lay at her side.

"I don't know how you could sleep at a time like this," she said, assuming that he had. Denny's big round face seemed to eclipse the sun at her window; she could smell the farm on his clothes, a pungent sweetness in contrast to all these metallic fumes. It seemed odd, and wonderful to her, that the future of this rough and self-reliant man would now be softened by a child.

He did not want to tell her about visiting the rivershore. "Why did I have to call Jack Hammond?" he asked. "He seemed surprised and not happy to be woke up."

"He's your uncle," she said.

"My uncle? I haven't seen him since before we graduated. I had to tell him my last name."

"S-h-h." She looked down at the small bundle, a pointy old man's face rimmed with a red rash, shrouded in a light blue blanket. His eyes were now closed, and when the nurse came in and took him to be checked over by the pediatrician he was so firmly bound in his blanket that he looked stiff, like a mummy.

"Why are you being so ornery?" Susan asked when they were alone.

He wondered why, and he looked around this hospital room, pleasant by any standard he could think of, a whiteness that spoke of hope and a busy hum that sounded like rest. He looked at Susan, drifting off in this borrowed bed; she seemed as haggard and puffy as his mother had when she was dying of cancer, perhaps even in this very same room, nearly ten years earlier. He had the sudden feeling that for families as well as hospital rooms, birth and death were really the same thing.

He banished these thoughts, wondering what was next and why it was taking so long, and then the door opened, and a trio of doctors walked in. One of them had a sort of pleased look on his face, as if he had just been proven right. When Susan was again alert, the doctors told them that the boy had cystic fibrosis, that his insides and lungs were already plugged, that he might not survive the week, and if he did he would probably not live long enough to enter kindergarten. The doctors—even the smug one—said it kindly, over the period of an hour or so, but that is what they said.

For the first months of his son's life, Denny could barely bring himself to touch him. He heard air passing through those small lips and pictured his lungs as blackened ruins dripping with tar. He watched Susan happily nursing the boy, passing her hand over the smooth contours of his silky head, luxuriating with the weight in her arms. It surprised him that she seemed, at these moments, so satisfied with her baby, despite all that awaited them. On late afternoons, when Denny came home from the fields, he usually found Susan and the baby in the kitchen. Sometimes, even before he entered the house, he could hear the deep jarring, thud, thud, thud of Susan's firm hands on the baby's back, the prescribed regimen for loosening what Denny thought of as the crusts and plugs of tar. The boy never seemed to mind this; Susan had learned how to drive the blow through the small body, and not to let it hit with a slap on his skin. But even so, Susan always ended the procedure by rubbing and massaging him, which made him giggle and coo. In time it became part of a sensuality between them, a kind of game, starting her hand down for one more blow, stopping just short and then folding into a caress, her broad palms covering his entire back. When Charlie had begun to talk, he said to his mother, "Smooth me," and Denny watched, almost embarrassed, as she passed her flesh—the inside of her forearms, her cheeks—over his body.

Back when Charlie was still a newborn, when the first untroubled and unknowing smiles began to appear, Denny prayed that this could all happen quickly, before he gave too much of his love, before he surrendered too much of his hope. It took almost to the end of Charlie's life for Denny to realize that this prayer was monstrous, that he had asked for an end of his own pain in the place of a cure for his son. Susan would make him pay for this. But by then Denny had also learned that of all the pain a human can endure, not allowing oneself to feel love is the worst; that denying love to oneself can destroy, from the inside.

In the hospital, during what they had all finally decided would be his last hours or days, Denny sat beside Charlie while Susan went home to eat and perhaps to cry in the solitude of the shower. Charlie was awake, naked except for a diaper, an oxygen tube, and an IV. He was breathing somewhat easily and his eyes were at rest on his father. Denny reached over to take his hand, and then began to stroke his small chest, running his fingertips around the cushioned indent of his nipples. Charlie smiled and closed his eyes halfway. "Smooth me, Daddy," he said.

"You okay?" he asked. "Can you breathe good?"

"Smooth me, please."

Denny dropped his hand down to the flat, starved stomach, to the navel that had opened too wide for the poisons that had been concocted from his parents' mingled blood. Charlie held still for those hands, rough and work-stained as they were, as Denny traced the lines of his body. "This is what it feels like here," Denny thought, rubbing the shoulder. "This is a tickle. This is a pat." He even lightly twisted a finger until the eyes reflected irritation and discomfort. He followed the sinews of each leg and then reached the top at the elasticized leg holes of the diapers.

"Smooth me, Daddy," said Charlie, and then Denny realized what the boy was asking him to do, or was it that Denny realized that there was one gift left to bestow? What does it feel like there? What will I miss? Denny could do this for a son, not for a daughter. As the boy, in dreamy rest now, lay still on his sheet, Denny parted the tapes of the diaper and put his hand back on his stomach. He traced down to the penis, to the tiny purplish tip, to the vacant scrotum. Denny looked up to Charlie, and the eyes were full of surprise and joy. Denny knew there would be no shame between them, even as the penis became erect, a slight nub of a thing. Denny imagined what he himself liked, how he liked to be touched, and he tried to do it, running his thumb up and down the bottom and closing the tip into his palm. He kept at it, lightly, not even wondering for a second what a doctor or nurse would think, and Charlie finally seemed to fall asleep, a rest full of gratitude, a relief from struggle, a life, as far as it went, full of joy.

In high school, Susan DeLorey's large frame, her big hands and feet, had made her seem heavy. No one would have called her cute, or ever did. "Solid," they said, referring both to her body and to her character. Perhaps marrying Denny, who spent most of his time in those days in bitter combat with his father, was one of the less practical things she had done. But Denny had settled down enough, taken an uneasy but consistent place as a partner in the family dairy, and he had begun to seem acceptable to the town ladies in comparison with the valedictorians and Boy Scouts who had long ago up and left their families with no warning. And since high school, the cute girls, the short and skinny blondes, the pert and sassy ones, had busted out of their blue jeans and peroxide, while Susan's age caught up to her strong-boned features, straight posture, and thick brown hair.

Susan worked as the electric meter reader for all "non-metropolitan" areas of the county. It took her half time, on her own time, and if someone invited her in for a cup of coffee and a doughnut, it was her decision to make. They gave her a car, with a whip antenna for its citizens-band radio, which flexed coyly as she drove from farm to farm. She had inherited this deal from her father, and it came with her to the marriage like a dowry. When Denny was courting her, after they had both spent their twenties dating others, she sometimes worried that it was the job he had fallen in love with.

After Charlie was born she contemplated giving the job up, and Denny had persuaded her not to. He said that she needed more than ever to get out of the house, and that she could bring the baby along, just as they had always planned. When Charlie died she was behind by two or three months on her accounts, and two weeks after the funeral she began to work overtime. For the most part, the customers, at least the ones that tended to be home during the day, were friends and admirers of hers. She came back from those first few days of meter reading in a car loaded with hams, and sticky buns, and roasted chickens, and pickled green tomatoes.

One evening, exhausted from a two-hundred-mile day, she was leaning across to gather some of these consoling gestures when she realized that her mind had slipped back in time for a moment, and that she thought she was reaching for Charlie in his car seat. She blinked past the illusion and saw that it was a casserole in her arms, and the hideous image of this food, and the shock of reliving the entire loss in a split second, gripped her in panic and she began to scream.

Denny heard her and came running out, opening the car door to receive her kicks and punches; he staggered off dazed from a good blow to his right eye, and she came after him, trying to hurt him. The hired hand saw her standing over Denny, kicking at him, and sprinted over the width of the farmyard. They called for Dr. Taylor, and he knocked her out with a full syringe of Nembutal.

Denny was off duty for the morning milking, and he was sitting at her bedside when she woke up. Their bed was a four-poster that had been her grandmother's, and Susan had made muslin curtains with ruffles to match the canopy. She had loved to sew before Charlie was born, lacy things, feminine touches of lace here and there throughout the house, as if to mark off a boundary for the odors and substances of farm life. Denny hadn't complained, but to this day, especially this day, he felt as if he slept in her private space. "How do you feel?" he asked.

"My head aches."

"So does mine," he said, rubbing his eye.

"I'm sorry, Denny." She cried rarely, and almost always for others, but this time, her face gripped by her large hands, her elbows clamped against her breasts, Denny could tell that she wept for herself.

"It's all over now. We can look ahead." He meant for these words to soothe, and he repeated them a few times.

He didn't feel he needed to argue the point and therefore did not put a lot of emphasis behind them.

She snapped up from her clenched recline and opened her full face to him. "It's that simple for you? You think now that Charlie's gone I'll just let you back?"

Denny knew what she meant, and he knew it wasn't fair, not entirely. She had all too easily let him free of the pain. She had gathered everything that hurt into herself, every one of Charlie's laughs and mangled words. That's mine, she seemed to say; I'm going to save that one for later. She had gone to each doctor's appointment loaded with questions, and night after night she studied the packets of information from parents' organizations and disease foundations. Denny could only scan these materials, squinting to screen the truths into a blur, looking for mention of a miracle cure. It seemed to Denny that everything in her mind had been backwards. Right up to the day Charlie died, she had been helping him learn his numbers and letters, and from the vantage point of an alphabet that would remain half unlearned forever, she seemed capable of staring into the deep almost cheerfully. Denny used to hear her teaching Charlie lessons for use later in life, and he had to cover his ears with his hands. Denny knew what Susan was saying, but it wasn't as simple as she made it sound.

"Are you God now, Susan?"

"No. There's no word for what I am. I'm a mother who lost her child."

Denny almost argued that he was a father who had lost his, but he didn't think the loss was comparable, at least, not in their house. He had often wondered what kind of father he would have been if Charlie had been healthy, and whether he would have behaved all that differently. Who knew? But this he could say to the mother who had lost her child: that he was a man who lost the person who would have become his best friend.

"I'm trying," he said finally, "to make you feel better. I want you to feel better." He spoke gingerly, not assuming too much, as if he was sharing her feelings out of kindness.

She heard these tones, and came bounding back. "Why didn't you love him? That was all he asked, to be loved by his mother and father."

Denny thought back to the last months of Charlie's life, and the last night at the hospital. How could she ask that? What could she be thinking of? He had no answer. He looked back at her blankly, and then said, "I'm trying to keep you from losing everything else."

She softened at this, even put out her hand to his. "Maybe you are. But there isn't anything you can do now." She got up, still in the T-shirt and underpants that Denny had left on her the night before. He looked at the curve of her hips, and he wanted suddenly to make love, to fall back into bed again like newlyweds. He could honestly picture this as something that might make things better, because it had been some years since they had really made

love. For many months after Charlie was born they had not
even tried, and then occasionally they had joined, and they
did not have to remind each other that there was fate in
their mingled fluids, they did not need to admit to each
other that when Denny was done and had withdrawn, the
cold drops of his poisonous semen burned on the sheet between them. They did not need to confess that any time
their flesh touched—a simple caress, a brush of the hands—
their thoughts bored deep through the skin and into the
code of damaged chromosomes.

Denny believed, as he watched his long-legged wife
walk across the bedroom, that they could leave this behind
now. He was ready, at this moment, with the sharp trem-
ble of desire. But she closed the door of the bathroom behind her, and then turned on the shower, and when she
came back out to the kitchen, she was dressed in her jeans
and was holding her account book, her No. 2 ½ pencils, a
flashlight, a can of Halt, and her thermos. "I might be late
this afternoon," she said. "I've got to go all the way to
Grangerfield."

Charlie died in May, and the long, buttery Chesapeake
summer moved through plantings, through the flowering
of the soybean plants toward the tasseling of the corn.
Denny threw himself into this work, this nurturing, but he
stopped the tractor now and again on the rivershore and
thought back to that unlucky morning, back to a moment,

now jumbled in his memory, when he had hoped that just beginning a life was enough to give it meaning. He made his turns on the tractor, and many times as he approached the riverbank he imagined what would happen if he simply kept going, down over the crumbling yellow clay and onto the pebbled beach, and then into the warm brackish ripples and out onto the sandbars, a mile or two into the Chester River before the water reached higher than his axles.

Susan was often away from the farm these days, even into the early evening, still catching up on her accounts, maybe, or hanging around with old high school friends to whom she'd never before paid the least attention. They all had babies, even big kids now, and after the difficulty of getting pregnant in the first place, and then Charlie, Denny could hardly imagine Susan wanting to spend time in someone else's happy chaos. But he had nothing better to offer, the gray silence of the house, the farm. As Susan said earlier in the summer, the real crop on this family farm was death. She said they weren't living there anymore as much as waiting to see who went next: the logical one—Denny's father; the unnecessary one—Susan; or the unexpected one—Denny himself. None of them had gained anything other than front-pew seats at the funerals. She said that Denny could not offer life to her, or she to him, the promise of it, and he knew well enough what she meant.

Evening after evening, after milking, Denny walked the length of the farmyard in the knowledge that the three men on the place, himself, his father, and the latest teenage hand, were all heading home to empty houses.

"It appears that your wife ain't spending too much time at home these days," said Denny's father on one of those evenings in August. They were standing in the roadway between their two houses, and the heat in the milking parlor had drained them both. He wasn't being hostile calling her "your wife"; he was of an older school.

"Her private affairs are her business," Denny argued.

The old man agreed. "I'm not anyone to pry. But things have to be managed, don't they?" This was an old point, his refrain from the years when Denny fought against him and against the endless repetitive details of the farm life.

"You don't manage a marriage like fences and Johnson grass, Dad. There's nothing I can do."

The old man gave him the same disappointed look that he had worn during those arguments in his teenage years, and Denny simply stared back, as he had done years ago. "There is always something," said his father, his eyes filling.

Denny nodded once more, and took those words home with him, across the broad lawn, and waited up for Susan to come back. It was seven-thirty when she pulled in. She was wearing her pale green shirt, with a new satiny scarf tied over the tops of her shoulders. She was carrying a sack of groceries, and she started to put them away, a bag of flour, a few cans of corned beef hash, frozen vegetables, without greeting him. He wondered if she thought of him anymore as she walked up and down the aisles of the Acme, what he liked; he could not imagine her putting much attention on shared meals, just on food, just on the common need to eat something.

"Sue," he said.

"Huh?"

"I'm not stupid. I'm trying to help." She seemed not to pick up on his invitation to confess. He added, "You can trust me."

She glanced over; the light was beginning to fade and neither of them had turned on a lamp. "I never said you were stupid."

"So where are we at?"

"I think we're just floating, as long as you ask what I think. I think I'm just waiting. I don't think anything that has happened all summer is real."

"I'm dairying," he stated. "That's real."

"Denny, as long as you ask—"

"I am," he interrupted, "I am asking."

"Well, I'm seeing someone. I'm seeing someone who makes me feel better."

The truth hit his gut; he could not deny that. But he could also not deny that he and Mandy Towle, in the occasional circling and looping through lives in small towns, had fallen together a few times over the years. "Why?" he asked.

She shrugged.

"Don't think I don't know why you are doing this. Another man."

Her eyes darted, but she only shook her head and told him that he could not possibly know what she was thinking.

"You're going to leave me behind, is that it?"

"Stop."

"Throw me off like a Kleenex?"

She did not respond to this right away, but continued to lean against the kitchen counter as she considered things, and she began slowly to get more and more angry, and Denny could not divine if it was because he had located her private truth, but at last she wheeled around for something to throw at him and came up with a canister of flour, which would have been almost funny, an explosion of white mist. Denny waited, readying himself to avoid the sharp edges of the tin, but after a few moments she put it down. "You asshole," she said, and went into her bedroom.

Denny slept, as he had been doing for a month or two, in the spare room. In the morning he leaned into her room and said, "I'm sorry. You can do what you like. That's all I wanted to say." But she was already gone.

. . .

Denny had a gift for machines. Before he was out of his teens, other farmers, even mechanics in town, began to seek him out to perform magic with a welder and metal lathe. He could do this, engineering answers not on paper but with his hands. The shop, from which these bits of genius came, was at the end of the barn complex closest to his house. It had been the granary, and the walls were still lined with rodent-proof tin. There was a single low window that looked down toward the creek, and in the afternoon, when the light came sideways, orange off the water, the grease-shined floor and tin walls glowed, a radiance that started at the feet and worked upwards as the sun fell. Early in Denny's marriage, his friends used to gather in the shop on winter Saturdays, drinking beer around someone's project, and the women gathered with Susan, cooking and drinking wine and Irish Mist, and after everyone staggered home and after he and Susan had made love a little on the dirty side, Denny lay back in the four-poster and thought the future was offering itself to him not in years, which no one could predict, but in seasons, certain and always new.

The winter Susan was living in town—she had moved in with her friend Beth, on Raymond Street, but spent most of her time in Chestertown—Denny closed himself into his shop. The maw of the vise stayed open, and the roller chest of Snap-On tools remained untouched. Often, at the end of milking, he went straight there, sat down in his cold

Morris chair, and stared out the low window across the lawn and to the creek, to the black winter water lapping at a brittle rim of tidal ice. Occasionally, when the weather wasn't too cold, Denny slept the night in that chair, and then, painfully stiff and foul breathed, he stole over to the house for breakfast, eating quietly as if she were asleep behind the thin partition of the kitchen. Early in the fall he went into town a few times to see Mandy Towle. They'd always liked each other, and she deserved a lot better than two failed marriages, one of them to a man from Ken County who was now in jail for house-renovation schemes that preyed on the elderly. She deserved a lot better than Denny, in these circumstances, which they both understood. She sent him home the last time, back to his shop, with a sisterly hug.

His father often stopped in to check on him, and occasionally sat down to talk. They stayed on dairying, for the most part, which wasn't a subject that held a lot more cheer than the remains of Denny's family life. Just sell the goddamn place, Denny said once; sell out and move to Florida. You deserve it. When his father hid his eyes, Denny knew the old man still hoped for the best.

"Do you think she's going to come back?" Denny asked. He knew that Susan had called his father once or twice.

"I expect what she's going through has a shape of its own."

Denny and Susan talked when they ran into each other in the street, and people could look out the windows of Todman's Insurance, or Latshaw's Jewelers, or Price and Gammon Hardware, and see them meeting like old sweethearts. The town was full of these almost-forgotten couplings, kids who had maybe once or twice fucked each other in his father's haywagon, or all winter long in her father's Buick, and what remained was a county full of people who treated each other like siblings, with the accidental intimacy of brothers and sisters who had shared the same bathroom. That's how it felt to Denny, meeting Susan on the street, and she seemed to want it that way, as if by wiping out their marriage she could eliminate her pain. Time, after all, had run out on them, had perhaps been running out on them for years: quality time, as the doctor said, had given way to the dry consolations of memory. "Until death do us part" would perhaps, despite love, turn out to be not long enough.

Denny brought these thoughts back into his workshop, these repetitive looping stabs at reason, all these variations on history. He tried to make sense of it, but he was finally bored by this hibernation, and as if in prayer, his thoughts had begun to wander. He could not say exactly from where or why the idea had come to him, but as the first stirrings of warmer weather came on the March winds, he realized that he had begun to concentrate more and more on the water, on the highways it offered, down the

Bay perhaps, and out to sea. His father hated the water; most farmers did. All it did was steal away land, a furrow or two between planting and harvesting in stormy summers. Kids went out on the water to drink beer. Watermen went out there to do God knew what. The Bay, that long question mark out there beyond Kent Island: Denny's father had raised him to believe the Bay was not only wet and dangerous but immoral, a slippery surface choppy with wasted money.

But the water called to Denny. It seemed to offer refreshment for his soul; it was as if he had recognized that he had been looking at only the land side of his life all these years, and had been missing what was perhaps the fuller half. He spent hours imagining boats, revarnishing and repainting the woodwork, overhauling the engine in the cooked odors of a clean bilge. He could not imagine why, up to now, he had never been curious about them. They seemed self-contained and sufficient, at once economical in space and extravagant with amenity.

In late spring Denny got in touch with the watermen at the Centreville landing, for whom he had repaired and built all sorts of labor-saving devices, and told them he wanted a workboat. The watermen were willing to help him, an intruder on the water, as long as he didn't tell anyone; when they found a good boat in Crisfield, they brought it up for him at night.

The following day, after knock-off, he drove it into the

creek and dropped anchor at the farm. His father, as Denny had expected, was standing on the creek bank ten minutes later.

"What in hell is this?" the old man yelled.

Denny paddled over in a dingy that had been thrown into the deal, and stood beside his father to admire the view. It looked like a destroyer, a dropping curve that started high and fixed at the bowsprit and then seemed to go on forever, like a view. "It's a boat," said Denny finally.

The old man was speechless; all the slack he'd given to Denny this winter, and this was what came of it, a boat? Like some goddamn rich Philadelphian? "Just tell me what in hell you mean to do with it."

"I don't know, Dad," said Denny. It was the truth. One thing Denny had learned during his winter months was to tell the truth. "Maybe I'll do some crabbing. Maybe you and me will go out and have picnics," he shouted as his father retreated back up the lawn to his house. "Maybe you and me will take it through the Narrows and down the Bay. Maybe we'll just keep going south."

For the next six or seven Sundays, through May and into the first heat of June, Denny threw himself into his project. He had never had much regard for watermen as mechanics: they tended to make repairs under way with vise-grips, and then forget about them when they returned to port.

Denny was delighted to have so much to do. His father continued to grumble for a week or two, but relented in the end to the point of putting an aluminum lawn chair under the shade of the lone mulberry tree and passing his Sundays on the bank. Occasionally they chatted with each other across the few feet of water.

One day in June, Denny had his head deep into dark thwarts of the hull, but heard the scrape of the lawn chair over the shells and pebbles of the bank. He assumed it was his father and did not come up for air for twenty minutes, and when he did finally it was Susan he saw. She was wearing a yellow shirt, which made her dark hair shine. Denny could not believe how lovely she looked, a wife on the shore awaiting a sailor returning from a long cruise. He poled his flat-bottomed dingy to her.

"I see you've got yourself a project." She was humoring him, as if the boat was childish, like electric trains.

"It feels good to be fixing something, for a change." He came down hard on the last word.

She looked over at him, and betrayed no emotions. She was wearing white pants and earrings, and Denny could smell the slight shade of her perfume.

"So who you dressing up for today?" he said.

She gave him no answer, no anger, no hurt. "Denny, a lot has happened to us, hasn't it?"

He shrugged, but it was clear to him that she had said this in preparation for something. Asking for a divorce, most likely. Get the unpleasantness over with, then drive back out to Route 50 and meet up with her accountant from Chestertown, or whatever he was, the person she dressed up for.

She continued. "None of it made much sense, did it? I mean, why did Charlie have to die?"

"Charlie's dying is the only thing that made any sense at all," Denny snapped back. "He had cystic fibrosis. Remember? What happened to him started happening from the moment he was conceived. It's a disease that began millions of years ago, some cell or something that crawled out of the water ass-backwards. Who the hell knows where it come from?" Denny realized he was shouting. "Charlie made sense, Sue. It's what happened to us in the meantime that doesn't make sense."

She raised her hands, almost as helplessly as if shielding herself from a pistol shot. "Okay. Okay," she yelled. "What happened to us. You want to whip my ass, Denny. Do it."

They looked at each other for a few minutes, across the oily shine of the boat's pistons, laid out on a rag.

"What I mean is," she began again, "that we've lived through some times I never expected, and we've done things I never imagined doing."

He shrugged, but she was right enough about that, right enough to say that everything she had done or thought since Charlie was born was contrary to logic, especially treating him as if he were to blame for it.

"I want to come home," she said. "I haven't seen anyone since Christmas," she added.

"Why?"

"Because it doesn't make me feel better. I still want to
die," she said. Her radiance, from a distance, had been an
illusion. She looked very bad, haggard and worn out from
within. Denny wondered if she had been looking this miserable all winter and whether he was just now noticing because he had turned the corner. But he did not want to feel
sorry for her yet. He got up, grabbed a handful of oyster
shells, and flung them in a spray far across the water. A
heron, feeding in the green shade of the other side of the
creek, took this as a sign that it ought to move on, and it
leaned forward, chest almost on the water, and then kicked
its long legs into the flapping of its wings. It skimmed slow,
unlikely, doomed, until it busted out into the sunlight and
headed out to the rivershore.

"Jesus," said Denny finally. "You've slapped me from
one side of this county to the other; I'm so bruised by you
that my piss is purple. There's some mercy in this somewhere, isn't there?"

She looked at him and nodded, and it was a look he had
not seen in a long time. She could not have been offering
herself as mercy, but as faith. Her eyes suggested, her head
tipped toward the house, but still, he could ignore these
gestures and they could vanish as if they had been nothing.
Denny did not know how to tell her yes; instead, he nod-

ded back at her, and if she expected the beginning of a caress on the way across the lawn, she did not show it. As they entered the bedroom, Denny was telling himself, as he had not done in many years, that he would soon make love to this woman in front of him.

She undressed with her back to him and turned to face him. He had forgotten the strength of her body, how broad and powerful she looked across her upper chest, how quick and nimble she looked at the tuck of her waist, how sufficient and frank she looked from the stretched points of her hipbones to the inside of her thighs. Denny had also undressed, and she gave him a little smile as they stood and looked at each other across the room. Her eyes dropped to his penis, and his to the patch of her pubic hair, and he pictured the outstretched arms of her tubes, the encyclopedia drawings with each ovary clutched at the curled extreme, and he pictured a line of eggs like pearls, some perfect, some flawed, ready to drop one by one into potential life, and then beyond. He pictured the grip of her uterus. She was looking at his penis, and he knew she also was tracing backwards to unanswered questions of that genetic disease, following on the long, circuitous route to his balls, where there were sperm cells by the billions, enough to conceive an epidemic.

They stood facing each other, naked as if new, and they understood that they needed far more than pleasure to make him erect and to open her to him. And with that understanding, pleasure did come to him, and she smiled again, this time more slyly, as he stiffened.

"Hello, Denny," she said, a joke from long ago.

He said nothing—this was as always—as they finally joined on the bed. He traced her lines, and searched for wetness and warmth, and very soon she was sliding one leg under him, and he did not ask what she knew about this minute in her month, and did not ask whether she had, in anticipation of this moment, driven over with her diaphragm in place, and did not ask whether she might want him to hunt through the bedstand for a condom. He allowed himself to be guided in. They rested for a moment, centered and tied in this way. He began to move, and long before he thought he was ready for an orgasm he was ejaculating inside her, and he pictured it not as a burst but as a showering, a mist like soft rain. Susan felt him come, and she too imagined what was happening inside her body, and it was a tumbling she thought of first, like the tumbling of an egg on its passage outward, and then—though she had not expected it—pleasure came to her also, and she pictured a wall, a brick wall slowly giving way to his continued motion and to the rhythmic encouragement of her own flesh.

Two months later, on a Sunday, Susan sat on the porch and looked across the barnyard to the water. She could see out the creek, across the wide mouth of the river to Eastern

Neck, and then, on clear days such as this one, across the dark line of the Bay and toward the smudged air of Baltimore. She knew Denny would be out there somewhere on his boat, but when she glanced up, she could not see him. She had a cup of coffee resting precariously on her thigh, and was reading the *Sun* in the streams of September light; she was warmed by the sensations and was happy to read the movie reviews, though she went to the show only rarely, with her friends Beth and Delia from town, and when she did, the other two spent the whole time making silly cracks about how beautiful were the male actors and how skinny the women.

When Susan thought about love and men these days, and about the past year, and about her son, her thoughts came ordered like a liturgy. It was necessary, in terms of fairness, for her to start always with her own general confession, with a listing of the things she had done. She did not think having an affair with Jack Marston was a particularly kind or clever thing to do. But Susan, as she considered these things, also had to go forward and admit that she had at least taken up once again a hope for the future because of it. Once she had confessed, she could proceed to a thanksgiving, to say that she was grateful that Denny had given her what he could, freedom, if not understanding; and then, because Susan did not blink at herself or at Denny or at the eternal pain losing a child had caused her, she gave thanks that Jack Marston had been there, because, in retrospect, without him she might have done something even less clever, killed herself, maybe. And finally, in her supplications, she could pray for the people in her life, for Denny's health and happiness, her mother and his father, for her sisters and their children. But not for herself, yet. She did not know what she wanted next; she did not know whether this move back, which she had done a few weeks after they made love, would work. She was waiting patiently for a sign. All she knew was that she feared nothing: she would never again be afraid, just a little hesitant, just a little reluctant to invite notice or comment.

She glanced down the length of the barns, silver in the morning light, and watched her father-in-law wash his car. He did this every Sunday morning in his milking clothes, before changing and then sleeping in front of the television. He had, last winter, called her a "loose woman." She had not argued with him; if she had, she would have told him that ever since Charlie had been born it seemed everyone on the place simply wanted her gone, and that she had done precisely that. She might have tried to explain to him that she had taken with her all those bits of Charlie's life that needed a resting place somewhere far from the farm. But during her marriage, she'd never argued with Denny's father, and he had a dim talent for her ways of thinking. Susan had always thought of her father-in-law as a man-child, and a girl-child at that, with a front tooth missing from her occasional frightened smile, a sort of waif trapped in an old man's rough and blemished body.

When Susan came back out onto the porch from filling her coffee cup, she saw that the old man had finished with his car, had walked down the long lawn to the water, and was staring out into the river. With his jug ears, his hearing had always been remarkable; he could sit in the barnyard and tell, from nothing audible to her, that the baler had broken down on the point field or that the hired hand was now in fourth gear on the Kubota and was heading for home. Perhaps he had heard Denny's boat coming in. It was a restful sight, the man under the water-side mulberry tree.

He turned slightly as she approached and then looked back out to the river.

"Is he coming in?" she asked.

"Sounded like it."

She took up her place beside him. The water was dappled gold; the slight onshore breeze was clean, clean but rich, like the air that came with the fresh-shucked oysters she used to buy for frying. She could smell the fresh milk warming on his clothes. "Do you see him?"

He waved his hand outward. There were several boats in view, indistinguishable to her except, perhaps, for the sailboats way over by the Narrows.

"What's he up to, with this boat?" the old man asked. He began by spitting out the words, but ended with a genuine question.

She stopped halfway around. "He likes being out on the water. He thinks it will save him."

The old man protested, this time with the beginning of a sarcastic snarl. "Save him from what? Seems to me what will save us—"

She put her hand out onto his shoulder and he stopped abruptly. They both looked at her hand, big, strong, a mother's hand, resting on his thinning frame, the white of her flesh against the green of his chino jacket. They both recognized that she had never done this before, that except for some early handshakes and the usual bumps in the narrow parlor when she filled in at milking, they had never touched in any way. A slight breeze, flavored with cattle, rose up behind them. It seemed almost miraculous for them to be joined on this small point of land. "Denny always took things hard," he said, after she had withdrawn. "That's all I'm trying to say."

Susan thought about Denny for a second, the man high in the tractor or deep, confident with his tools, in the guts of the combine.

"I don't suspect you know that he was a soft boy. He liked to be held by his mama."

Susan had guessed this, but it made tears come to her eyes anyway.

"By the time you knew him, he was fresh enough," said the old man. He pulled out a handkerchief—a washrag they used to clean the teats before plugging them into the milkers—and held it out for her. She knew what it was, still damp with disinfectant, and she took it. "He was even softer than his sisters. One year he planted a flower garden over behind the equipment bays and he made bouquets and vases of flowers, you know, to give. It was a girlish thing to do," the man said, sounding as confused now, and as unsure, as he must have been thirty years earlier, a dairy farmer with a boy who loved flowers. "The teachers were partial to him."

Susan listened, and waited for more, wanted these images to do their job, feeling as if these tears could be the ones she had been waiting for all this time.

"If I had it to do over again . . ." he began, and then stopped. Neither of them needed him to describe how he had reacted to this child.

"What?" she asked. She brought her hand to her face and felt the oily release of mucus on her fingertips.

"Sometimes I look at him and I catch a glimpse of that soft boy. In his eyes, I expect. It's like he is asking me for something. I always figured he would get it from his own family, but that wasn't to be. I always hoped you could make it right."

"I—" she said, ready to tell him she couldn't do it alone, but he talked past her.

"I wish you could see the boy like I do," he interrupted.

He had ended on a sort of question, a plea perhaps, and now seemed to want her to respond. But she no longer had anything to say, no answers to a father so troubled by his son, no apologies to a father who loved his boy. They waited as she blew her nose, and they both turned their stares out to the water, as if worried Denny might sneak up in his boat and overhear this conversation.

She did not want her thoughts to turn toward sorrow. This had not helped her. To ward off the impulse, she thought back for a moment to herself as a schoolgirl, without blemish, living in the uncomplicated glow. She had always liked herself best in her Brownie uniform; because the older girls wore precisely the same costume, Susan didn't feel so awkwardly big and tall. Perhaps at some point, in the past year or two, she had let the girl in the brown dress out of her grasp, let her fall away as if disappearing down a sweet but deep well. She no longer felt, as she had in her younger adulthood, that she was living as two people, the girl and the woman.

"I sometimes think all of us out here just gave up a little early," she said.

"Speak for yourself," he said, but it wasn't said harshly. It was more of an absolution than a retort.

"Oh," she said. "I've got plenty to confess. I expect that goes without saying."

The old man put up his hand to stop her. He turned to go, but seemed reluctant to leave this brilliant September day and to let this conversation stop. He looked at her, and made her realize that he believed the next step was hers.

"Charles," she said. She rarely used his name.

"What?"

"I can't fix everything. You know that. It's not as if I have any magic." She did not know why she was so certain that this was what he wanted.

"I'm not asking for magic. You've come home. That's enough to keep from offending the dead," he said finally. "The boy and my wife." He began to walk away, heading up toward his house. Susan found herself waving to him as he departed, and then turned quickly to see that Denny had entered the mouth of the creek, a tall weather bow, unnaturally, stunningly white, plowing toward her out of the molten sunlight.

She waited on the creek bank, sitting in the dry autumn grasses. Denny caught the mooring ball and was making the line fast. He seemed in a good mood, his skin a golden reflection in the tea-colored water. He looked fine as a waterman, big-chested over the low sides of the boat. Suddenly, as she looked upon this graceful scene, from deep in her lungs came a wave of joy, a relief as if for the first time in years her whole body had relaxed. She could feel it in her chest and in her shoulders. Could it be, Susan wondered, that this morning, this very moment, was what she had been waiting for, that mourning would end with the same abruptness as it had begun, begun with the words, out of a sleep, as any parent fears it most, a strange doctor saying *Wake up, wake up, it's about your son Charlie.* But

Charlie isn't even born yet, she had told herself as she roused; how can doctors be waking me up with bad news about Charlie?

"Hey," Denny called out as he poled close.

"Sh-h-h," she said, putting a finger to her lips. She did not know why it was necessary for him not to talk. She watched him struggle for a second or two with an answer, perhaps even an angry complaint about being cut short when all he was saying was hello. Since she had moved back they had been careful with each other, and had not probed for feelings, and had sat silent for phrases or thoughts they did not understand. Asking for explanations would have done no good. Susan wished that her life and her marriage were that simple; she could hardly remember the time when it was, when words took care of what words were supposed to and touch handled the rest.

"Can you be with me here for a minute?" she asked.

He sat down beside her on the bank. He had moved a little beyond her, and when she turned in her seat to face him she saw the old man watching them from the patch of grass in front of his house. The three of them hoping for a peace or for a change, depending on her. It was maybe not much of an audience. Out of all the people she had known in her life, her own family, her girlfriends, the boys and men, her electric company customers, out of the planet's billions, only these few, this assortment, looked to her. Was that enough to make any of this worth it?

"A real pretty day out there," said Denny, Denny the soft boy, the one who loved flowers.

She moved over closer to him, her knees parting the grass as if she were still in school, still looking up at Denny from her spot at the senior picnic. She took his hand, spread it out between hers, attempting to flatten the natural cup of his palm with her thumbs. She could feel the pulses of blood, stunning bursts of life-giving pressure.

"It may be over," she said. She held her breath, waiting to see how this would feel, once said. A *V* of geese honked overhead, a cow bellowed angrily from the holding yard, a school of small fish breached the surface in front of them in a gravelly shower. She was glad to have these other voices join in with hers.

"I'm hoping so too," he answered.

She wished, for a moment, that he had not used this word. Of course she had hoped for many things, beginning with herself, things done and things left undone. She had hoped to be a mother, but for the moment, once risked, it was better to put that hope aside. Especially with the new knowledge and choices that could be revealed in a drop of her fluid, conceiving life seemed to have much too much to do with death. She had hoped not to be still thinking in such terms, but she was. She had hoped— maybe "pretended" would be a better word—that Denny could suddenly become someone quite different, starting with what she had learned was a slight defect, a trivial speck of dust, located on the long arm of his chromosome 7. Denny could also be more communicative, less defensive, more open to suggestion, less interested in sex, more interested in love; he could not have that palm-sized birthmark on his left flank and his breath could be nicer when he awoke. Hope, in other words, seemed a little beside the point for Susan.

He said, "It didn't seem anyone did anything wrong, anyway. That's the thing. Neither of us did anything wrong."

She quieted him once more, and this time he seemed content to sit with her in the grass. She could see Denny's father disappearing into his house; she could see the inevitable lineup of cows beginning at the far gate, drawn by the pressure of time as they measured it. She felt Denny remove his hand from its splayed captivity, and she looked down to see him moving to pick up one of hers. She would know everything when he did. There was no way for either of them to lie on this one: the moment had come, almost five years reduced to a slight clasp of his hand. It could be a little too tight and then relax too abruptly; a sort of halfhearted greeting, something for a cousin, something to be gotten over. That would mean that they would live out their lives side by side, but that it would never be sweet again. His grasp could be too loose, a kind of forgetful drape, the kind of thing you do to keep your balance. If so, they would drift apart in a year or two, and perhaps he would lose the farm and start drinking. Or he could run his hand into hers, flatten it against her palm and find the fit for his fingers; he could search and then, slowly, take what she gave him, herself, and he could draw the two of them together, and this is what she expects, and it will be enough, not perhaps for every man and every woman, but for her, and for him, for now.

ABOUT THE AUTHOR

Christopher Tilghman lives with his wife and three children in central Massachusetts. He is the author of a story collection, *In a Father's Place,* and a novel, *Mason's Retreat.* His stories have been anthologized often in *The Best American Short Stories* and in other anthologies in the United States and abroad. He is the recipient of numerous grants and awards, among them the Guggenheim Fellowship and the Whiting Writer's Award.

ABOUT THE TYPE

This book was set in Galliard, a typeface designed by Matthew Carter for the Merganthaler Linotype Company in 1978. Galliard is based on the sixteenth-century typefaces of Robert Granjon.